# ENVY

# Envy

# JUDY CORBETT

ISIS
LARGE PRINT
Oxford

First published in Great Britain 2007
by
Ebury Press, an imprint of Ebury Publishing

Published in Large Print 2007 by ISIS Publishing Ltd.,
7 Centremead, Osney Mead, Oxford OX2 0ES
by arrangement with
Ebury Publishing, a division of the
Random House Group Ltd

**British Library Cataloguing in Publication Data**
Corbett, Judy
    Envy. – Large print ed.
    1. Envy – Fiction
    2. Teenagers – Fiction
    3. Large type books
    I. Title
    823.9'2 [F]


        ISBN 978–0–7531–7902–4 (hb)
        ISBN 978–0–7531–7903–1 (pb)


Printed and bound in Great Britain by
T. J. International Ltd., Padstow, Cornwall

For Peter

# Acknowledgements

Special thanks to Judith Chilcote,
Hannah MacDonald and Miranda West

# CHAPTER
## ONE

We were girls together, Isabel and I. That's where it all began. Two girls from the same village — in reality, different continents. She from the big house, Critchley Hall, I from The Shack on the Lower Road; or so I called it. And it did matter, even though she said it didn't. She liked me for what I was, she said. I felt like a shell she'd picked up on the beach. I felt like a keepsake.

We met on a rock — a volcanic accident — the kind of rock sailors are shipwrecked on; though there was no water, only a beautiful vale webbed over with hedgerows full of birds. She was sitting on one side of this rock reading a book and I was sitting on the other, also reading a book. I thought I was alone until I heard her yawn; a yawn like a small mammal sneezing. A very curious sound it was. I turned my book words down onto the grass and went to investigate from what creature the sound had emanated. And I found a girl whose body reminded me of a seed-pod just on the verge of bursting. I said, "Hello," and she looked at me through a sulky brown fringe. She was pretty. I wished I had been born pretty. Her cheeks were the colour of sliced bread.

Of course we'd seen each other in the village: I, the urchin child gathering fruit in the summer lanes; she, always behind tinted windows so the whiteness of her skin in sunlight surprised me. But now, face to face, we prowled around each other like tigers, tails ramrod straight with fur all upstanding.

"I've seen you around," I said.

"You live on the farm," she said, "your stepfather rents it from my father. You belong to us." Teenage girls can be cruel. She had every idea how much those words would wound. I raised up my chin to try to dampen the fire that flared within. She saw. She blushed. She closed her book, indicating her regret. And that little slip of thoughtlessness was enough to put me on the winning side.

"Look," she said. "I didn't mean it. Why don't you come for tea?"

At The Shack on the Lower Road, tea was a main meal at five o'clock. At Critchley Hall it was sugar and spice and small triangular cuts of bread without crusts. We sipped tea that tasted of burnt twigs out of pink-and-yellow cups that had butterfly wings for handles. There were landscapes of reassuring peasant scenes hanging on the walls. Through a square of rippling glass I watched a gardener skim leaves with a net off the garden pond. The room was smaller than the child in me remembered. I'd been here once before.

"I've upset you, haven't I?" she said.

"Of course not," I replied; her attention raising me moth-like to my feet.

"Then say I'm forgiven."

I played the moment for dramatic effect. I stroked my chin, then tapped the ends of my fingers onto their reflection in the tabletop. "I forgive you," I said, without conviction. She smiled with relief, leaving soft indents where her fingers had been in the surface of her sandwich, then amazed me by putting lemon in her tea. We talked. She told me which moisturiser she preferred; had I discovered a certain kind of nail varnish guaranteed not to chip, had I ever hennaed my hair, and I stared at her in disbelief, my mouth just a little bit ajar.

Later, she showed me her bedroom. She told me the colour on the walls was gardenia. Her bed was heaped with a white cloud of pillows and suspended above the headboard was a dainty canopy of lace that reminded me of the Virgin Mary. I went to her dressing table and fingered the necklaces she wore about her neck. There was a musical box made out of shells that she said had belonged to the daughter of an emperor. It was filled with a tangle of beaded purses that her parents' friends had brought back for her from around the world.

"Try this," she said, spraying my cuff with Eve's Delight. It was a wicked, molesting scent and when I put it to my nose I knew that nothing would ever smell the same again. It smelt rich and I was tired of being poor.

I thought of my bedroom, the room I shared with a couple of stepsisters of the Cinderella kind; though they weren't especially ugly and I was no aspiring princess. My mother was my real mother whom I loved and I had a stepfather who preferred me to call him uncle.

The bedroom we shared looked out over a paddock full of geese. The sound of them made me think of the potato famine — a lesson from school that had stuck. Squares of newspaper wedged the wardrobe doors shut. Three small iron-framed beds were pushed to the furthest corners of the room, as though contagion lurked in the horsehair mattresses. Every night I fell asleep to a landscape of watchful faces staring down from the cracks in the ceiling. We each had a little chest of drawers in which we hid our private things beneath a pancake-stack of knickers. But privacy was all in the head: a state you strove for but never attained, like love or receipt of it. The broken lock on the bathroom door put pay to privacy. Every morning the gulls came back and settled on the granary roof, charring with the geese, and every night the sheepdogs rattled on their chains like weary ghosts.

Isabel must have noticed the dragging corners of my mouth. She said, "C'mon, let's go and find my dad."

We'd gone up a back stair and having walked along a landing framed with hunting prints we now came down a front stair. There were gilded putti on the ceiling of the stairwell. My plastic soles made shaming little thwacks on the marble stairs. There were logs piled up in a wicker basket like parcels of butter waiting to be melted in the flames of the drawing-room fireplace. Such demonstrations of grandeur made me want to act the clown. To my surprise, I opened my mouth and made a sound I'd not heard myself make before. I meowed like a cat that has a bird in its mouth and the echo burnished the walls with my longing. Isabel

4

looked shocked, then laughed, then drew in her breath and sent up her own whines with mine so that our cattish voices carried upwards like smoke, like mating butterflies. She grasped my hand and launched it into the air with hers, in the way of cheering footballers after a goal. I was not impressed but I went along with it, for she looked unbearably pretty with her blackberry eyes and deep dimples in which a porcelain dove might have laid a clutch of small golden eggs. I hoped her prettiness would contaminate me. I hoped I could be changed. Even then I was aware of the rot that lay within.

We found Daddy polishing the flank of his sports car in a converted loosebox, where the growl of a V-6 engine had replaced the soft whinnies of Irish mares bred for their broad hindquarters.

"Hi there, Sweet Pea," he said to Isabel, with his eyes on me. "Are you two having fun?"

"We're going down to the peach house," said Isabel. They made eye contact: pupil to pupil. There was something going on between these two. Something dark and normal. I felt out of my depth, and not for the first time. I offered him a primeval little pout to hide my gaucherie and the direction of his polishing changed from landscape to portrait. He wore the bottom half of a pinstripe suit, with his tie tucked in between the buttons of his shirt. Though it was a weekend, I wore my school jumper — at fifteen it was a garment I was proud of growing out of.

They then gave a little performance entirely for my benefit while I kept quiet. A not very funny joke from him; a whining "Daad" from her; a cat's tail swipe with his duster aimed loosely at the back of her bare leg.

"Bring me back a plum, girls." And Isabel grinned.

Later. We lay in the tall grass — The Rough — as it was called, where the mower couldn't reach and ate the fruit we'd picked in the glasshouse. I liked my fruit slightly green and unripe; Isabel liked hers brimming over, preferably with red juice. She bit into a plum, and I heard the skin snag on her teeth and the juice flooding her mouth and spilling onto her lips. She said, "I love this weather," tossing her plum stone into a stand of cow parsley. "If I have to die, I want to die in the sun," and she fell back into the grass with her arms above her head. Two wood pigeons with bloated undercarriages flew above our heads. I could feel the heat bouncing onto my legs from the span of bricks in the high garden wall.

"I'll remember that," I said, and we laughed whilst watching a thrush pull a worm out of the lawn.

"Come again tomorrow and we'll swim," and then she got up and I saw a latticework of grass had imprinted itself on her thigh.

Isabel is able, I told my cat when I got home. Isabel is a belle. I made a list of some of the things she had and I did not: beautiful handwriting, a family pew, pasta kept in jars. In the right-hand column I made a list of some of the things I had and she did not: chapped lips, burgeoning eczema, caged rabbits.

That night I thought about what it meant to be me; looked carefully at myself in the mirror of the wardrobe. It was the first time I'd really noticed the features of my face. I was instantly forgettable even to myself. I saw hair the colour of gerbil fur and so fine you could see through it to the paleness of the scalp beneath. I had a centre parting as broad and angry as a sutured wound. Green eyes: passable. Pale skin with an emerald tint, as though I'd stood in a draught too long. I willed myself to have poor eyesight so that glasses would animate my face. There was already too much of me. Isabel, on the other hand: the perfect shape of her, her eyes so round and dark, like rich puddings you could sink a finger into; the way she still smelt sweet at the end of a hot day, the residue of an expensive cosmetic lingering. I cut off my scent-saturated cuff with pinking shears and kept it in a box marked SPECIALS, a word I'd scratched into its lid with a compass point years before.

In bed that night I tried to sleep but I couldn't get her out of my mind. It was like watching an advert for Isabel: Isabel modelling Isabel in a series of delectable poses; Isabel standing next to her father's car with blue sky behind, asking if I'd like to go for a drive, saying: "What a beautiful day, too good to waste — a crime to waste a day like this." Then Isabel in a snowy landscape with fur around her face, saying: "Do you ski? What am I saying? Sorry, of course you don't." The snowflakes piling up on her eyelashes and she closing her eyes because of the weight of them, and I wanting to knock off the snow as you would off a hedge, because I'm terrified they'll lose their shape, their beautiful ski-slope shape. But I'm not really there, she's been talking to an empty space. I am invisible behind the camera. *I am the camera* and when I touch myself in this restless half-dream of mine I feel the boxy, square corners of me, and when I try to walk towards her I find I can't because my legs have become tripods.

I missed the swimming engagement with Isabel the following day. Something happened which stood in the way of me going. As I was leaving for Critchley, the sheepdogs came in and ran under the kitchen table. They were called Pepto and Bismal and their markings were identical though on opposite sides, like a nut that has been halved. They sat trembling and licking their lips in fear. They were kept on chains in a dark shed and their excrement formed a crust upon which mould grew. Moments before, I'd heard my stepfather shouting at them in the field. They were rounding up sheep but the dogs wouldn't obey him, wouldn't do what he told them to do, which was to round up the ewes in a clockwise direction. They kept going wide of his stick and took no interest in the sheep, only having eyes for him and the pain he might inflict.

Their eyes were wild, as wild as his, and their tongues lolled out of their mouths, like pink ribbons long enough to tie into bows. The sheep scattered across the field. Then there was silence; my stepfather's voice like an engine cutting out in the sky. The sheepdogs came running into the kitchen. There were swipes of mud on the lino where their paws had slipped, and drips of blood where they'd cut themselves jumping the barbed-wire fence. Then the engine tripped into life again and the shouting was suddenly with us in the kitchen. My mother gripped the edge of the ironing board and told me to stay out of the way — to "vamoose", in so many words; but I stayed pressed up against the worktop, the smell of warm, singed clothes, an itch inside my nose.

He came in and threw his cap onto the table. It landed on a scald mark where a hot kettle had rested. Two-thirds of his face was red from sunburn and fury, and the remaining third, where his cap had been, was white like an egg. I imagined I had a spoon large enough to crash through the shell of his skull; I imagined the yolk mixing with the red and the green that would result. The dogs cowered and bared their teeth at him. His face was bloated as if he'd drowned but come to life again. He took his gun from the cupboard. My mother turned her face away and so much was said in that sideways glance: it explained how things could be accepted and borne just by looking the other way. He dragged the dogs outside by their collars, with his gun pointing at the sun. They were pedigree and worth money but it was not enough to save them.

At times like these I imagined my own father fighting him. He had died a long time ago and I had no memory of him. But in my imagination my father always beat him. Always knocked him to the ground, and afterwards shook himself down and straightened his tie, and turning to me said, "You'll have no more trouble from him now."

At times like these I fantasised about exchanging my family for another. I thought of Critchley with its clean solid walls and glass lampshades, and I knew I'd found the family I wanted in exchange. I thought of Isabel and how, right at this moment, I should have been pulling the cover off the swimming pool with her. "The last swim of the season," I could hear her say, "make the most of it, the weather's turning colder." But it would still be one of those remarkable days that you never forget, when the leaves and the buds and the small things look so intense, look coloured in, the miracle being that no crayon has strayed over the edges.

I imagine her body like a shapely bullet entering the water and how she doesn't appear for ages, and I look at my watch and see the outline of her, corrugated by the movement of the water on the bottom of the pool, and I look around for someone to call, panic stopping the words from coming. Then finally her head breaks through the surface of the water and she's already laughing and saying: "That scared you, didn't it? I can do a minute underwater. You can time me if you like."

After the shots had been fired I went outside to look. There were drag marks in the gravel where the dogs had pulled against him. They lay one on top of the other like crossed foxes on a pub sign. Pepto's leg still twitched. He'd been my favourite because he was the runt. A trickle of blood emerged from his nose. My mother came out and told me to be thankful it wasn't one of us. But I couldn't be thankful; I couldn't be thankful for something that had kept me where I was. I stared at the dead dog and thought about the word "step" in relation to father, and how an alternative meaning was a surface to be trodden on.

The following days passed in a haze of empty longing. Critchley was on the surface of everything I touched, like a film of dust. It was behind my eyes and in my ears and there was no silence any more; there was only the sound of the fountain falling on the head of a stone cherub. My stepsisters watched me closely sensing a change in me, a small chink of possibility in an otherwise closed facade. They were always searching for the weakness, the hairline crack that would fracture and expose the heart of me. It was jungle law, the weakest died, and to give away any part of yourself meant victory to the other side. I was careful. I only allowed myself to think about Isabel at night when no one was watching. But in the dark, I sensed my stepsisters' knowing faces smiling at each other; their whispered voices uniting against me like a chain-link fence.

A few days later a car drew up behind me in the lane and I heard Isabel's voice say, "Leave me here. I'll walk back." The car door closed with a clunk. I turned and saw her walking towards me, her steps short and deliberate like a dancer's.

"Why didn't you come last week?" she said, "I missed you." (The idea of being missed by Isabel: the flick of a switch and light after dark; an impossibly tight bottle top that finally unscrews.)

I said, "No reason. It just didn't seem like the weather for swimming."

"But it was a beautiful day, better than any we've had all month."

I shrugged my shoulders, took off my jumper and tied it round my waist. "Today looks pretty good," I said. "Shall we do something?"

"Like what?" she said.

"I've got an idea. Come on, I want to show you something."

We walked up the lane under the chestnut trees where the conker husks had been flattened on the road and the white meat of the fruit had tarmac showing through it. Although it wasn't hot, Isabel picked up a leaf and fanned herself with it. The countryside was wide and open as though we were the only people in it: Isabel and I climbing over the stile, her tap-dancing shoes clicking on the chicken wire covering the steps. The track we followed to the mouth of the cave was caked and hard, and she kept stumbling and reaching out for my arm. And I laughed and made fun of her unsuitable shoes, but was secretly impressed at the disdain she showed the countryside by wearing them.

We reached the cave. The opening was small and the floor sandy. There were the remains of a campfire with rocks around it and charred pages from a magazine scattered in with the ashes. The green on the walls was greener than anything that grew outside. There was a sound of dripping somewhere deeper in the cave and the walls were wet and silvery like cheeks after tears.

"What an amazing place," Isabel said, and we walked further in and I knew being inside the cave gave her the same feeling as it gave me: that sometimes-safe, sometimes-scared feeling, like being kissed by a friend of the family you didn't quite trust. I knew by the excited look on her face that she had never been anywhere quite like it before. The cave had been a secret place for me; somewhere I went to when the pieces didn't fit. The air was cold, clean, almost a drink when it touched your lips.

"They go for miles, these caves. They found bones here in the twenties and evidence of man. Listen to this," I said, moving towards a deeper chamber. "Sabre-toothed tigers and woolly mammoths. *Mammoths, mammoths, mammoths,*" my echo drifted through the darkness of the cave. This was the best of it as far as I was concerned: the way it spat out a paring of your voice. It was like shovelling coal into a furnace to give out heat. Isabel clapped her hands, delightedly. The trees whispered outside, and she took a breath and began to sing. "And what did the baby do now? And what did the baby do now? *Now, now, now.*" She sang it gently as though she had once been rocked to sleep by the song and had never forgotten it. The voice came out of her mouth like a liquid that poured slowly. As soon as she began to sing I knew that it had been a mistake to bring her here. I suddenly saw the cave for what it was: a cold, damp, dripping space that smelled faintly of urine, where tramps sometimes came to sleep and foxes to eat prey.

"Shush, shush," I broke in, stamping out the flames of her song. "*Shush, shush, shush.* You'll wake up the *bats, bats, bats.*" Her voice trailed off. "I have to go," I said, and left her standing in the cave fingering the fissures in the rock face. I knew I would never return to this place that had once meant so much to me.

Everything had changed. Isabel had spoilt the cave for me because I knew in my heart that she was a better secret than the cave itself. I looked back and saw the pale shadow of her watching me go; Isabel standing there like the answer to a question I had no words to ask.

She sent me a note but I didn't receive it in time. My stepsisters intercepted it and gave it to me three hours after I was supposed to meet Isabel in the cave. They thought it was funny and laughed until the tears rolled down their fat, flushed cheeks. I felt like a nail being hammered into wood. It was another petty victory for the victors of casual cruelty. I held the black-edged card in my hand. It was old sympathy stationery and, I suppose, not inappropriate under the circumstances. The slight purplish tinge of Isabel's rich black scrawl and the sweet, inky smell: "*Meet me at 2*" — and she'd drawn a picture of a cave with giant-sized bats hanging upside down.

I snatched my coat off the back of the chair and ran out of the door. I didn't stop until I reached the gates of Critchley. Me in motion: noticing everything about the hinges of myself and the surprise that my breasts moved, actually made themselves felt; pertly impertinent beneath the cable weave of my jumper. A blind, furious run on the surface, but beneath the me of me an awareness that the bondage of childhood was almost over. Freedom and the taste of toothpaste in my mouth. The hedgerows rustled as I passed and it seemed as if all things were in flight. I'd never been to

Critchley uninvited before. I didn't know what I'd do when I got there. There were cars parked on the edges of the drive and the tinkle of distant voices. I hesitated, momentarily dazzled by the glare of sun on glass. People, mostly women, were standing on the lawn tipping teacups to their lips. A small marquee with open sides had been erected near the house. I walked off the drive and into the shadow of the trees and the ground was no longer smooth but crunched beneath my feet, as though biscuit crumbs had been strewn before me. I walked towards the house, out of sight, through a patch of shrivelled vegetation that smelled of chemical spray. Bursts of laughter exploded in the air. The back door was open: I went in; the house was empty. In the hallway there were scissors and ribbons on the floor and strips of unused Sellotape stuck to the edge of a table. I peeled one off and a sliver of wood clung to its sticky side. An unfinished cardboard sign on the floor said "Plant Sal". I looked out at the people in the garden: at their moving mouths with bits of sandwich inside. The smell of damp, walked-on grass filled the house. There was no sign of Isabel.

I walked up the stairs, tired suddenly. The light in the stairwell was soft, expectant, like watching a feather fall from a great height. I imagined myself living in this house: what it would be like to pull doors into frames that fitted snugly, the slight squash of air in the rooms making your ears pop. What it would be like to actually see yourself in the veneer of doors, in all sorts of polished surfaces, even the backs of forks. I imagined running a finger through clean, dirtless dust that lay white under beds. What it would be like to set a washing machine to come on at night or to own a set of chairs too valuable to sit on, or to walk on a carpet that showed stitches, that someone had actually sewn together with thread. Imagined one whole room with nothing in it but a table-tennis table.

I'd reached the end of the landing without realising it. The house was quiet. Isabel's bedroom door was closed. A curtain billowed out of a window. Some of the windows had blinds covering them. I looked down at my hands. My fingers were playing with a small object. It was a miniature hourglass. I must have picked it up without noticing from the table at the bottom of the stairs. I held it up to the light. Tiny grains of sand clung to the inside of the glass. I turned it over and the grains flowed slowly. Outside the clouds too, I noticed, seemed to be moving slowly across the sky as though aware of some inner injury that would hurt if they moved too quickly.

Where was Isabel? There were patterns of light on the wall. One tiny piece of coloured glass in the window and the wall was speckled with red light; it was as if someone had been shot against it. The air around my face smelled of warm rug and newish paint and some other scents from outside: clean washing (almost indistinguishable from fresh air), a nearly-out bonfire and something sweet: pastry perhaps, pastry with melted icing on top. I looked out of the window and saw Isabel selling cakes at a cake stall. She was passing change to a woman who had purple hair, the colour of an ailing bluebell. She was laughing at something the

**16**

woman was saying: something had amused her, or perhaps she was just being polite and was laughing at a joke that wasn't funny at all. She touched her throat, played with her necklace. The woman asked her about the stone in it. "It's topaz, I think. Yes, topaz is yellow, isn't it?"

I smiled too. I felt at home in the house and at ease. Being there felt so natural, so simple and fluent: meant. Any moment now Isabel would look up and see me at the window and I would wave, and she would wave and she would be delighted to see me, absolutely genuinely delighted to see me: the words she'd use. With her eyes, which were laughing, she would ask me to come and rescue her, *pleeese*, with three e's in it, because Isabel was the kind of girl who would use three letters when one would suffice. And I would disappear from the window, then suddenly appear at her side, as though I'd held my breath and swum through the bowels of the house. We'd ignore each other momentarily while she was theatrically polite to an elderly woman who had a swipe of blue eyeshadow across her forehead. She'd say, "Don't mention it" and "Here we go", passing a carrier bag full of scones over platefuls of other cakes. And then she'd turn inwards to me and hug me and say, "Thank God, you've come just in the nick of time. Death by cake and old ladies."

"I was looking for you in the house. I'm sorry I didn't come to the cave. I got held up."

"Never mind, you're here now. I'm absolutely genuinely delighted to see you. Let's leave this," she said waving to the cakes and flinching when the back of her hand hit a wasp. And we crept away from the stall taking the largest chocolate cake we could find, leaving everything there, even the tin that held the money with its lid off and the roll of sticky price tags that would never get used.

It was only later, much later, as I was walking back along the road that I felt something hard and sharp sticking into me through the lining of my pocket. It was a leg of the miniature hourglass. I must have lain on it in the grass by the river, yes, at the moment Isabel had said the word "comparison" in connection with the hundreds and thousands on top of the cake. "Let's for the sake of argument draw a comparison," she'd said, reaching for the cake. I remembered now. Turning over on my stomach, the weight of the hourglass giving way; the hundreds, perhaps thousands of grains of sand in the hourglass escaping and the air in the hourglass escaping too after all those years. I dribbled a thin golden thread of it all the way back to The Shack on the Lower Road. The sand on my fingers still tasted salty.

We saw each other as often as we could. Sometimes Isabel would come and look for me on the farm. I hated that more than anything else; more even than my stepfather whose favourite pastime was to remind me that I wasn't his. I didn't want her to see me among the straw and the turnip peelings. I didn't want her to see me. She never spoke to the rest of my family and when they saw her leaning on the gate, waiting, they would laugh and nod towards her saying, "Your little friend's here." At those times I loathed Isabel.

Then one day I was picking potatoes. It had started to rain but two rows had already been lifted out of the ground. The lights were on in the little red-brick Methodist chapel we attended at the top of the field. I imagined Margaret with her harelip polishing the altar candlesticks. Blistered cream paint around the iron radiator pipes. The heads of the lilies painted on the pulpit reminding me of textbook genitalia: Book 2; fig. 1. The light was fading; a fine spray of cold rain grazed my face and my fingers closed around the clods of wet earth in which lay a buried spud, if you were lucky. I was thinking about the archipelago in the Aegean Sea, a place in a book: imagining the clear blue water creeping over the shore, like the merino blanket my mother pulled up beneath my chin at night in a haze of winey breath. I imagined the gorgeousness of warm sand between my toes; a gull or two riding the thermals; the rocks like a bank of spilt pearls upon which I could lay my back. A shape on a map. For a second it made the rain feel warm, but the smell of the potato blight revived me with the strength of smelling salts. I wheedled out the potatoes from beneath the grey earth and dropped them into my bucket. My back grew stiffer, my head heavier.

And then I looked up and there was Isabel standing in the open gate. She was smiling. She held open a coat for me. I could see the mouths of the armholes beckoning like tunnels I knew I must go down. Longing and thirst blistered the inside of my throat when I swallowed. I dropped the bucket and walked towards her. I walked towards her through a jeering crowd but I kept on moving, placing one mud-logged wellington in front of the other, keeping my eyes fixed on the beckoning armholes of the duffel coat.

"You shouldn't be out in this rain," she said. "I came to get you."

"Yes," I said. I plunged my hands into the armholes as though I was diving into a ravine to save myself. The smell of wet wool from the coat and the rotting carcass of a dead sheep in a ditch nearby engulfed me.

"There's tea and a hot bath at home."

"Yes," I said again. The feeling of absence and bliss rose up in me like yeast, its spores multiplying until I could no longer shut the door on it. Her presence was more persuasive than a ringing phone. Isabel led me towards the lane that led finally to Critchley Hall.

All my favourite books had big houses in them. The sharp-cornered reality of my own life; the soft-paged fantasy of hers. The possibilities Isabel's friendship presented were like small flowers opening on speeded-up film. There were plenty of clues. All anybody had to do was read my face for the full text.

I did not go home much after that. And nobody seemed to mind. My mother was glad I'd found an escape route. "You go for something better," she said. "You'll get nowhere if you stay in this stink." She was piling clothes into an open washtub, the smell of dirty laundry and budget washing powder rising up from the dun-coloured water. Earlier I'd found a bottle of spirits in the left leg of my wellington boot. I pushed it back under the slate slab in the pantry. My mother deserved anything she could get and who was I to wag the finger? I suspected there was a small part of her that was glad to see the back of me. The intensity of my stares depressed her. I knew too much: I was the only one who'd seen the colour of her insides and that gave me a right to judge her as a mother and enumerate her shortcomings as freely as I liked. As far as I was concerned, having married us both into this hole she'd earned herself *nuls points* on the electronic scoreboard.

I filled up my rucksack with the sum total of my possessions. And then filled another with books as my departure to Critchley Hall was based on the pretext of a temporary stay to study for exams. But we both knew I would probably never return. I took down my collection of second-hand postcards off the corkboard on the wall and fed them into the wood stove, watching the flames bend the cathedral spires and shrivel the palm trees to ash. "A nearby village with an attractive market. Weather sunny but not too terribly hot. Regards to all." The words curled as though written on the backs of autumn leaves.

Casting a last look around the kitchen, at the smoke-blackened ceiling, the kitchen cabinets made for a good price and now showing it, the row of tomato plants growing in yoghurt pots on the windowsill, the box by the stove where pet lambs were taught to suck — the cut-price, 20 per cent off, feel of it all — made me nostalgic for none of it.

I said farewell to the fake willow pattern on the dresser and, of course, to my tabby-point Siamese. She lifted up her chin for me to stroke in the place that only

I knew well. I whispered: "I'll come back for you," into an ear I'd nursed through canker. She gave me an accusing stare and then began to follow me out of the door. The sight of those determined ears moving up the path tore me into shreds like an old love letter — ripped, I felt, into feint-ruled islands of remorse.

I walked round the side of the house and let my rabbits out of their cages. I opened the doors wide. They wouldn't go at first. I had to drag them out by the scruff of their necks and put them down on the grass. And then they ran — with woodshavings clinging to their stomachs and ears flat on their heads — across the shorn grass, through the hedge and into the field beyond.

I walked back to the house. My stepfather had a sheep on its back and was scraping maggots out of its foot in the big open-sided shed. They dropped to the floor like spilt rice, each fleshy grain giving me new resolve to close the door on this whole sordid little interlude that was my childhood. Best years of your life, a tall, bearded adult had once said to me while stroking the blonde down on my cheek. Best years of my life? I'd repeated, puzzled, for it didn't bode well for the rest of it. My stepfather shouted after me that he'd shoot the rabbits if he saw them in his crops.

I picked up my cat and deposited her in my mother's arms. I said farewell again. The washtub went into spin and drowned out the last words she ever uttered to me as a child.

★　★　★

Isabel's mother, Phileda — Mrs de Burgh to the rest of us — was piercing the necks of tulips with a needle to make them lift up their heads, when I arrived. We were in a hallway with chequerboard flags and gilt-framed mirrors all around. I moved diagonally across the floor, carefully stepping only on the white flags like a pawn on a winning strike. Her face was the colour of delft between the blue, her nails the colour of the blood clot in my mother's left eye. She had the air of someone recently emerged from a small jar with a screw top. Her eyebrows were pencilled on like Pierrot's.

She called me darling: "Ah, darling, there you are," and I was flattered, until I realised she didn't know my name. Her voice creaked lasciviously like the rope of an old hammock slung between two trees. "I'm so glad you've come to stay. Isabel badly needs a friend. She spends far too much time alone."

"It's very kind of you to have me, Mrs de Burgh," I said, with roses in my mouth. "I appreciate the time to study." No I didn't. I was quite especially clever and knowledge of the textbook sort seemed to stick to me. I could read it once and have it in my head under house arrest, leaving my mind free for other distractions.

I looked her full in the face. The clear blue of her almost transparent eyes registered not a flicker of recognition. Could she truly not remember? Could she truly not remember the look of wounded pride on the child's face or the shame on the mother's? My hand throbbed in remembrance, fingers crushed tight like a fan in my mother's grip.

"It'll help if I have you with me," my mother had said. "The wealth will always take pity on a child." Memory came as involuntarily as a bowel movement. We are shown into the breakfast room with the pleasing little peasant scenes all around and are told to wait. The seat of the Chippendale chair upon which I sit is as expansive as a stage. My mother keeps pulling her skirt down in an effort to hide her big heifer's knees. She takes a handkerchief out of her bag, spits on it and tries to scrub away my frowns. She does this almost every day. The deep indentations in my forehead must leave shadows. They won't come off, I explain, I was born with them. She smiles like she smiles every day when I say this.

Mrs de Burgh enters the room in a haze of pearly light. She is wrapped like a gift in flowered fabric and smells like an angel must. She is all silk and seaweed in the diaphanous glow of the lamplit room. Her head tilted slightly, she alights like a robin on the back of my chair. My mother snaps her handbag closed and begins to rise.

"Please don't get up." She waves her down like a pawing dog. "How nice of you to call. You must take a walk around the garden. The magnolia is at its best just now. George will give you some boughs to take home if you wish." I feel her breath on the back of my neck like the blow of butterfly wings.

She makes to go on but my mother, without realising that it is impolite to talk about incidents appertaining to real life, interrupts and says quickly, quietly, "My husband is cruel to me. I have to leave him and I must find somewhere else for my daughter and I to live. Could you help us? A tied cottage on the estate, perhaps? I can pay rent. I even have references. Here I've brought them."

Mrs de Burgh reels backwards, as though my mother has pulled a gun from her bag and is pointing it at her heart. All I can feel is the elastic in my knee socks cutting off the blood supply in my legs, like the rubber rings that make the lambs' tails fall off. (Though it hurts to be disloyal, I'm with Mrs de Burgh on this one. I want the gloss, not the real text. I want to put the horrid detritus of life through a strainer in order that I may sup only on the pure essence: the best that money can buy.)

But my mother persists, "Help us, please," she says. "We have nowhere to go." I feel my backbone become longer, one long bone that will drag like a tail on the ground for the rest of my life.

There is a moment, before the process of kiln-drying fixes Phileda de Burgh's features into granite, when I believe she softens. I turn and gaze up at her, expectant, and the gaze from those same blue eyes rains down upon me like silver coins. I reach out and touch her hand that is draped like a glove on the back of the chair. Veins so blue and pronounced they remind me of Dark Age earthworks after snow. The hand recoils. A cloud covers the sun. Wake up, child. Wake up! What were you expecting: a happy ending? She draws herself up as though she is about to deliver an aria. Her small breasts rise like dough. I expect song; I receive injury. She says, "I'm afraid we've nothing for you."

But what about Gorse Hill or Red Cottage? What about the numerous, empty, bone-shaken huts we could make better with our brooms and our pots of magnolia? A cave, an attic, a space beneath the turf would be better than The Shack on the Lower Road. I could be Romulus and Remus, both; my mother the wolf, and we could be happy living beneath the bristly sod, eating beech mast and elderberries.

Thanks to Phileda de Burgh's lack of social conscience, we ended up in a mildew-stained caravan amongst the geese and chickens in the garden of The Shack on the Lower Road. It was no more substantial than a house made out of beer mats. It stank; it wept a sort of fungal cancer from its plywood pores. It was like sleeping between two tiers of a sponge cake. The ignominity: better the cave and the heathered air; better the oak tree and its protecting canopy. I lasted two nights; my mother lasted three. And then we slunk back into The Shack on the Lower Road: me with my sleeping bag; she with her empty, clouded glass. We were given a sneering welcome; I'd like to say it was downhill all the way after that but I've never been one for talking things up.

Thanks, Mrs Phileda de Burgh. To this day her empty cottages decay, easily, like discarded cardboard boxes on a motorway embankment.

We got up to leave and she led the way out of the door. Composure had settled like a dove on her face once more. In the glazed porch, rich with the scent of warm jasmine, she said, "I do hope you'll come again." She touched me lightly on the shoulder as though I should be grateful. "Do have a look at the garden on your way out and be sure George gives you some tomatoes to take home."

"Say thank you to Mrs de Burgh," said my mother. But I kept my head down and focused on the whitening that was beginning to flake around the laces of my plimsolls.

# CHAPTER
# TWO

It was Sunday night. Sunday night at Critchley Hall, Isabel informed me, meant scrambled eggs in front of the television in the morning room. A small disappointment. I'd wanted ludicrously heavy spoons, Georgian preferably, and napkins that cracked when you shook them open. This was the part I never understood: pick a room, any room, and out of choice they'd plump for the smallest interior; the plainest lame Jane. Not a flash of ormolu to be seen anywhere. The walls were beige; the curtains were drawn. The scent of roasted dust belched upwards from the electric fire. We sat harnessed into our chairs by supper trays waiting for "Mastermind" to begin, like inmates of a nursing home. Anyone peeping through a chink in the chintz would have purred at the sight of such a cosy family scene: mother, husband, daughter — and, if you narrowed your eyes almost to closing you might have said, sister. I had the cuckoo fledgling's feathers sprouting in my armpits.

The one concession to a plump wallet was the bottle of Pomerol that Geoffrey de Burgh kept close to his right hand. The dust on the shoulders of the bottle spoke volumes for its vintage. "Like a glass?" he said, seeing my eyes fall upon the label. "I think these girls are big enough for a drop, don't you, Phil?"

She said, "As you wish," with her eyes fixed rigidly upon the screen. The lights had dimmed, the black leather chair was illuminated and the drum roll reminiscent of an execution had begun.

He gave us each a crystal glass into which I dipped my sanguine nose. The wine smelt of damp dust long settled beneath antique Turkey carpets. It was not the colour of blood from a rose-pricked finger; it was the colour of blood in a transfusion bag. It contained within itself a meaty, crimson redness. I put it to my lips and took a sip, and suddenly every country of the world was jostling for *Lebensraum* on my tongue. A mouthful of tastes burst forth in one loud firework crack: salt, lemon, sugar. That one enrapturing sip contained the flavours of them all.

I was delighted by my first five-star experience. Isabel wrinkled her nose, said it was sour and passed it back to her father. He was amused by my delight in his wine, but it was the kind of amusement you get when you discover your dog has a penchant for grapefruit segments. He topped up my glass and gave me a wink.

We were hushed to silence by Phileda who was floundering under the lifetime achievements of Isambard Kingdom Brunel. Every wrong answer provoked a howl of derision from Isabel that was infectious in its succinct estimation of her mother. I tried to camouflage a giggle with another sip of wine. But a loud nasal snort escaped me, betrayed me even, and Geoffrey de Burgh turned his whole body towards me in a condescending twist. I felt trapped under his fastidious gaze like an insect he'd caught in an upturned glass. His legs were tight in his trousers. He was not what you might call attractive. Childhood freckles had united to form continents of brown skin across his face. He'd mostly gone to seed; but seeds can be propagated anew in warm houses and he'd kept himself in shape with a five-step workout every morning. But the thing I loathed most about him, the thing that really gnawed at my entrails was the way he made me feel about myself. In short, like a pan of pulpy apple left too long on the stove. I felt poverty glide out of my pores under his gaze: my cheap hairslide, school shoes worn at the weekend, torn skin around my nails, shiny skirt in spite of the care I'd taken to iron it inside out. He made me feel as if the whole of my life was something worth recovering from. Forever after, I hated tall men and all their landed claptrap.

Eyes still upon me he said, "Let's see how well our little milkmaid does on general knowledge, shall we?" I thought: I'd beat you to a pulp with a long bat for that, if I had my way. I thought: you'll pay. Even Phileda threw him a questioning glance. All eyes were on me, and all I could hear were the branches of the magnolia tree scratching at the window. I sensed the wind was cold outside; that the sheep with their hacking coughs and grass-stained knees would be sheltering in the old railway carriage up on the bluff; that the salmon would be lying low, barely moving, stomachs brushing the algae-coated stones on the river bed.

30

And then the voice from the television said, "Your questions start now." It's only some stupid quiz I told myself.

It seemed like a long time, like a long string of questions but it probably wasn't. I can only remember one of the questions now. "Name the artist who painted this picture." It was *The Scream* by Edvard Munch. An old favourite, in fact. It was tempting to see myself on that pier with my hands over my ears, my nose two pinpricks of black and my mouth an elongated egg of despair. I very nearly lost my calm, but just in time I saw Geoffrey's mocking smile spread across his face like a stain waiting to signal my failure with a ragged flourish. In time that smile would goad me into behaving with absolute surety.

The point about the quiz was that I got five questions right in a row. That was the very point. I got five right in a row before Geoffrey started talking over me and walking in front of the screen, offering everyone (except me this time) more wine.

"Oh, bravo," crowed Phileda, giving me a slow clap.

Isabel said: "You clever girl," as if she meant it.

Geoffrey said in a loud aside: "Some people can be so lucky with the questions." He looked exactly as I knew he had looked as a child after a hard slap on the lower leg, bottom lip pushing out as though he was pulling tongues inside his mouth. Isabel and Phileda started to laugh and I began to laugh too, as if I would never stop, until I was hanging over the side of the chair, though I knew quite well we were laughing about entirely different things. I had the sense of a vague, warm triumph spreading in the pit of my stomach. It would be a while before I felt it again.

A small bed had been erected for me in Isabel's room. After a long spell spent luxuriating in the en suite, I finally emerged and threw myself beneath the duvet. This was a new experience altogether, which I never learned to like. I was more the sheet and itchy blanket type myself. It was the weight I liked. The blankets holding me down like earth on a grave, happily preventing me from rising up to walk with the dead in dreamtime. I propped my head up on my hand and watched Isabel scissor out of her clothes. A white teddy bear with deep-buttoned eyes and a perplexed expression on its face stared down from the top of the wardrobe. She talked whilst she stripped and I counted eleven knots of bone running down the length of her spine.

"My mother really likes you," she said from inside her T-shirt.

"Does she? I wonder why?"

"She thinks you're clever and a good influence." We both laughed at that.

And I said, "Why are you laughing? Don't you think I'm a good influence?" Her head emerged through the neck of the T-shirt and she gave me a sly look.

"Only time will tell," she said, and threw herself heavily into bed.

"Anyhow, I really like you being here."

I asked her about the dead of the house: those who had once walked the corridors with candles raised to light the way. She said she'd never thought of them, never let them in.

"But why not? They're here you know. Apparently, ninety per cent of all household dust is made up of human skin — some of which the dead have left behind. We probably breathe it in."

"Oh, don't," she said, pulling a pretty face. Her room was situated in the old part of the house. Moonlight came in through the little diamond windowpanes and made patterns across her bed. I could just see the soft mounds of her legs rising up beneath the duvet and her hair spread out across the pillow, like dark strips of metal on an anvil waiting to be beaten by a blacksmith. I knew that even in sleep she would be beautiful. That she would breathe through her nose not her mouth, that her bare left arm would fall back against the pillow in the tragic way of 1940s filmstars; that the pose would come naturally to her, but not to me.

"Do you like your father, Isabel?" I asked into the moonlight.

"Not much," she said. But I knew it was only a bluff to make me feel less alone. It was clear she adored him.

I had the worst night's sleep of my life, what with the duvet and the fountain sounding like a burst pipe dripping behind the wainscot, and otherwise silence from the garden; no birds. My mind wandered in the blue light. Apparently, when Leonardo da Vinci saw a caged bird, he would buy it and set it free: white wings unfolding in a grey sky like nail parings. That was the kind of thing money could do. It could buy a bird's freedom. Strange how birds were always doves in the imagination.

Listening to Isabel's soft breaths in the semi-dark, I thought of my mother who once owned a mynah bird called Joey. Some wag taught it to speak, but it mimicked my mother's voice. Everybody laughed when they heard it because it defied nature in its capacity to speak, and aberrations of nature are often funny. But I thought it was grotesque. Not because of the excrement and the flies that buzzed around the putrefying grapes in its bowl but because it had stolen my mother's voice from her. She never sounded the same afterwards. She was always trying to make herself sound different from the bird.

I once left the window open, hoping it would fly away. It sat on its perch, head tilted, watching me with a blue eye pierced by a pupil that resembled an ink drop. But the truth was it had been born in captivity and so had no nostalgia for freedom.

Neither did my mother then. She was content making rugs out of pieces of coloured rag. She said it took her mind off things; I didn't dare ask what. Later she moved on to something more ambitious: she embarked upon a patchwork quilt constructed out of small hexagons of coloured fabric. It was to be something for my bottom drawer in later years, assuming I would make the same mistakes as she had. She sat and stitched in front of the fire, with the quilt multiplying and spilling over onto her lap like honeycomb. It reminded us both of happier times and sad times too, though nothing so sad as what we'd ended up in. I stacked up the paper templates like chips on a roulette table, passing them over when she asked with a nod. The quilt was made from a ragbag of bits: pieces of maternity dress that my blind, kidney-shaped self had once disfigured; an apron; a striped wynsiette nightie; the skirt of a suit with grass stains down the back. The trouble was, my mother, by her own admission, claimed the only taste she had was in her mouth. Consequently, the colourific value of the quilt roamed through a miasma of dusky pinks and murky lemons. I was somewhat relieved when she scorched it in three places with a cigarette and it ultimately followed the sweating corpses of dead sheep onto the bonfire. Now, of course, it was the one relic of hers I wished I still possessed.

Isabel moved in her sleep. My mother was the past for the moment. Badgers. Half-sleep. The sound of a metal gate closing somewhere in the dark.

"Isabel used to love water when she was little," said Phileda in the car the next day. "D'you remember, we used to check for webbed feet when you came out of the pool. You loved that." We were going on a picnic to the lake. It was Geoffrey's idea. We were in the old Rolls. He'd had the steering column fixed and wanted to take her for a spin. The smell of petrol fumes and polish was so strong you could taste it; it was a texture in the mouth, small balls of crushed taste like peppercorns or capers.

"Next you'll be getting the photos out, Mum," said Isabel, raising her eyes to the heavens and spiralling her finger against her temple to indicate lunacy. She sat back and ran the little silver cross that was around her neck up and down on its chain. She had a white shirt on, crisp, clean, as though there were still cardboard in the neck of it. It wasn't cold but she stretched across and pulled a travelling rug over our legs, tucking it carefully round mine as though I were a jewel, a prize, something worth protecting. Such an act of consideration was a new one on me; it was embarrassing, but I liked it and did not recoil.

We drove through the outskirts of the village. "What a pity the new houses are spreading," said Phileda, "and such ugly ones at that!" I had an image of them airborne, a virus of small houses being blown across the land. Cow parsley whipped the sides of the car and uphill the engine moaned; a change of gear was like a gasp for breath. We crossed a narrow bridge; there were people throwing sticks into the water. When they saw the car they waved, all smiles, and I wondered why they were happy for us, why they didn't hate us for driving a car like Geoffrey's. The road got narrower. We crossed a cattle grid then drew up at the first gate: a stretch of lake was just visible beyond the tumble of trees, like the tail of a prehistoric animal disappearing behind the hill.

"Open the gate for your mother, Isabel," said Geoffrey.

"But Dad, I've twisted my ankle," said Isabel.

"Off you go, shirker." The banter continued.

Isabel dragged herself out of the car. Phileda pointed to a flock of Canada geese that were flapping overhead, oblivious. The gate had come off its hinges. The three of us sat inside the car and watched Isabel struggle with it, the dragging of rusted metal across the ground, the bottom bar come loose. Then Isabel mock cross because nothing was working the way it was meant to: then Isabel laughing and whining, and shouting, "Dad, *come on.*" She knew we were all thinking how beautiful she was; how beautiful the solid colours of her dark hair and white shirt were against the blue. Even Phileda smiled, suddenly attentive. She was like a picture; too commanding to take your eyes off. Finally, the gate was open and she took a bow. And for the first time in my life I was gripped by a feeling of being a part of something, and yet I had never been so apart, so singularly different from those around me. I was reminded of the last time I'd visited the lake, under different circumstances: sent to look for a lost sheep in the rain — ha, I the lost sheep, searching.

I was the first to laugh when Geoffrey did the jokey thing of driving off just as Isabel tried to open the car door. Isabel didn't think it was funny. She sat down on a low wall next to the road and wouldn't move. Geoffrey reversed. Phileda wound down the window and said, "Come on, darling, he was only joking." But she sat there and ignored them and attended to her split ends, a small girl in a big landscape commanding more attention than the moon, which was still out in the morning sky. It took Geoffrey a full two minutes to persuade her back into the car, during which time she didn't speak.

Once she was back inside the pouched interior, she said in a microphone voice with a fist against her mouth: "This is your flight attendant speaking. I'm sorry for any delay caused but we've been experiencing difficulties with an unruly member of staff. Disciplinary action will ensue and your journey will be resumed as soon as possible. Have a nice flight, ladies and gentlemen." Geoffrey slapped the back of his hand playfully and the car moved forward. She threw her head onto my lap and feigned sleep, and I made a little plait in her hair that stayed there for the rest of the day.

We drove to the edge of the lake. There was a boathouse and the waves lapped in and out of it as though its walls were cupped hands, catching. Phileda spread a rug on the grass while Geoffrey unpacked the hamper. Isabel sat on the running board of the car and watched. She asked what kind of trees they were, the ones that were growing in a circle on the far bank. She knew nothing of the country; she treated it as a playground, a sandpit in which to get dirty. I said they were Scots pines and they often grew well in wild places such as this. But before I could finish she was up and hugging her mother from behind.

"What have I done to deserve that?" said Phileda, dropping the cheese knife and grabbing Isabel's arm, delightedly.

"You don't play tricks on me like Dad does." The midges gathered in clouds above our heads. Something broke the surface of the water and the ripples echoed in rings, and spread and spread again. "I'm not hungry," Isabel declared.

"But there's all this food," said Phileda.

"Diane will eat it all, won't you? She's a growing girl." She threw me a slice of apple and laughed at her own joke.

Geoffrey smiled that sly, lizard's smile and lifted up his newspaper. I walked to the edge of the water and skimmed a stone. I wondered what it must be like to be the flame other people warmed their lives around; to be listened to even when you made no sound.

The next evening we walked in the garden; it was too warm to be indoors. I let Isabel talk. She told me she had won cups and ribbons for running at school. I hated people bragging about athletic prowess. Only people with no brains bragged about how fast they could run. I guessed it was something she'd picked up from her father, wishing she had been a boy. How hard you could hit a ball really meant something to him.

The garden was very still and quiet. It had just rained and the leaves looked polished. There was a fig tree growing against the wall of the coach house whose leaves were as broad and flat as the faces of Chinese children. Large raindrops collected in the green creases and rolled like tears into our waiting mouths. The lime trees rustled and there was no moon. It was suddenly dark. I loved the world much more at night and the thought of the animals that worked the night shift watching us from the undergrowth. I knew that had I been alone I would have slipped into the darkness as into a bath and the night would have swallowed me whole. All the warm smells fumed from the earth: the stainings; the seepings; the phosphates; nitrates; potash, absorbed and released again as vapour.

I could sense Isabel's dislike of the dark; her every step stiffening and slowing down the further along the path we went. But she wouldn't dare admit her fear to me. I took that as a sign of her burgeoning dependence upon me.

"Hear that?" I said.

"What?" said Isabel.

"That sound of breathing."

We stopped on the path and listened.

"There's nothing," she said quickly.

"Fine. That's all right, then," I said. I knew there was a cottage on the other side of the walled garden, near some abandoned beehives. Another tied cottage; tied in a binding knot to the ankle of Critchley Hall. An old man lived there. He'd kept the kennels for the hunt in his day. I knew him because I sometimes did the village paper round. He gabbled like a goose to himself. I could always hear him in the back room when I pushed open the door. The dark, flagged corridor, the wall of tobacco smoke and the scent of cat piss, though never a puss for miles around. It was said he trapped strays and fed them to his hounds to save on dog food. Inside, a sepia version of the world; every surface varnished by a film of nicotine. *The Light of the World* nothing but a dull shadow on the wall. Him jabbering about Moses from his armchair and the state of the trains. Me clutching his copy of *The Field* to myself like a shield, scared rigid. Two packets of Players, bulking out my pockets to help his emphysema along. His skin was kippered by tobacco; his jockey's frame, I suspected, as light as a lampshade.

I found myself wondering if this man had ever been young, had ever been beautiful. It helped to take my fear away. There were old photographs of lads on the walls: strong lads, looking as though they had conquered the world, with their shirt sleeves rolled up above the elbows and caps pulled low over their eyes. I picked him out. The one in braces, clutching a short-haired terrier. Same hollowed cheeks; slightly bulbous eyes: the last parts of the body to age. I didn't know that you only truly value something after it is lost. But I learnt it then, casting my eyes between the bright-faced youth in the photograph and the wizened husk of the man in the chair. I ran out panting into the blinding light, full and sad, a racing tip ringing in my ears.

There was a holy well in his garden. A compound of water contained between high stone walls. Roman, some thought; others thought it was a danger to cattle and ought to be drained. Mouth parched, I knelt down by the little stream that ran from it and put my lips to the clear, bright water. I drank a deep, sweet draught; cleansing, I thought. But when I raised my eyes I saw three dead puppies bobbing in and out of the extraneous weed. He'd drowned them for good and for providence. I remember the dark tips of their ears and their damp fur, crimped, like a 1920s hairstyle.

I heard him shouting from the back parlour, "Put money on Everlasting Life. Put money on the two-thirty at Newmarket."

I knew all this and consequently there was no fear for me. But it was different for Isabel. She hated being near the cottage. Underneath, when you stripped the bark off the girl, she was as superstitious and as reverent as the villagers. They still called her Miss Isabel in the manner of forelock-pulling servants and she, as a mark of feudal affection, called them Joe and Ted and Lewis. I soon embarrassed her into noticing the anomaly by asking her whether Miss Isabel would care for a biscuit or would Miss Isabel care for some ketchup on her anchovies. Soon after, rather than risk a name exchange in front of me she began to avoid them. And they in turn said she was giving herself airs — about as damning an appraisal as you could get in a small village.

The villagers thought that Jack the Hunt was a crazed old lunatic and this notion had cross-pollinated on the feet of gossiping insects into Isabel's consciousness.

"Don't let's go near," she said, in a half pleading way.

"But we're here now," I said. "And if we don't have a look, you'll always be scared."

"I'm not scared," she said. "It's just so dark and I might fall."

"You won't because I'm here to catch you. Now, let's just have a look." I grabbed her sleeve and pulled. A button gave but she didn't notice. She was like a doll I could manipulate, her limbs soft and malleable, her will completely submissive. There was no point going up the front path. I wanted her to see him through the window: to have a good look at the sort of squalor I was used to and she was not. There was suddenly a moon and I could see the light reflecting off the little stream. A dog barked and a chain rasped against some metal railings.

"I'm going," said Isabel.

"No you're not. We're here now." Again she let herself be pulled towards the lighted window. She was like the tide washing in and washing out against her better judgement.

We were walking in a flowerbed. I could feel the brittle stems give way and the soft sink of my shoes into untended soil. It was late summer; there were still insects about. They bit and flew about our heads. The house was silent like the quilted quiet that presages a disaster. We peered in, making goggles of our hands against the cold windowpanes. And there he was: Jack the Hunt sunk down in his chair like a teabag in a cup, same colouring too, with his head resting on his chest the way all old men sleep in chairs. Isabel gasped at the room. She saw quite innocuous things: one hovel is much the same as another — a room rotating through various degrees of dirt and orange peel, stacks of yellowing newspapers, feathers, clinkers spilling from the dead fire like scree, saucepans encrusted with last month's meals, tins — all empty with their jagged lids up. I was behind Isabel, leaning over her so she couldn't escape, so she had to look and see. A little grime and gristle and the goosebumps soon erupted on her arms. There was something about Jack the Hunt that evening that gave even me the jitters. He sat there hunched, unmoving, like the old man he really was, rather than someone with the allure of a bogman recently exhumed. There was something black moving around the corners of his mouth. The shimmering heat of the evening; barnacles of sweat clinging to the underside of my arms; Isabel's fear hot against my stomach.

I realised what had happened before she did, which gave me time to pick up a stone from the flowerbed and hurl it through a windowpane. As I did this a great cloud of something like soot erupted through the broken pane. Now this was a moment to get excited about. This was a moment of acute sensation because, yes, the old man was dead and this was not an eruption of soot exploding in our faces but bluebottles; bluebottles pouring out of him like black-suited airmen piling out of a burning plane.

"Oh Jesus," I heard Isabel say. "Oh Jesus, no."

The gamey smell of him slowly coagulating in the warm kitchen bit like an insect sting, but it took you right to the heart of things. It took you to the core. All flesh, after all, is grass and the mean parody that is the rest of it.

Isabel, in a swoon reminiscent of some flouncing diva, fell backwards and because I was behind her, I caught her. I'd fantasised all my life about being able to faint like that, especially for the purposes of avoiding school assembly. I'd always thought how lovely it would be to emerge from a white sleep with faces gathered over me, mouths set to cooing. "Such a delicate constitution, poor thing." The next best thing would be to die of TB in a white nightgown with a handkerchief bespattered with my own red raspings. Alas, I was too big-boned for those sorts of shenanigans; too hefty for a poetic death.

So I looked on with unwilling admiration at the sleeping beauty who'd landed in my arms. I dared a kiss even — her forehead irresistible like the smooth surface of a diamond. I wondered how long this beauty in my arms would last in a spot of role reversal: if she were condemned to a new life at The Shack on the Lower Road, where the soap was hard and cracked and never wore out. That love and hate could lie side by side like this should have brought me to a bewildering conclusion. But it did not. I propped her up against the side of the cottage and went to get Geoffrey.

It was twelve days before Isabel fully recovered from her encounter with Jack the Hunt. She claimed she had swallowed several bluebottles and the thought that they had once fed off the insides of the old man made her vomit until her own insides felt stripped to below the grain. Mercifully for her, exams were long since past and summer stretched ahead like a bolt of fabric laid down especially for our amusement. Or that's how it seemed to me.

Isabel was a demanding patient. She took to her bed because she felt too queasy to stand up. And reluctantly I played the willing nurse. Phileda was mid-menopause and had been banned from Isabel's room since the beginning of the holidays. When together they knotted easily like fine hair, so the best policy was segregation. My inclination was to lie around, occasionally moving from the foot of Isabel's bed to the window to watch the herons descend with javelin beaks to gobble the carp from the fountain. The world outside seemed entirely composed of midgreens and russets: first the lawn and the curtain of mature trees that edged it, and then beyond the ha-ha to the nibbled park where sepia cattle swung their tails with jaws rotating. The heat slowed us down. We slept all night with the windows open, listening to the tone of slaughter in the vixen's call and the owls responding. Sometimes I would get up and embark on a star-counting exercise. At times their randomness was loathsome to me. In the day boredom broke through our pores like sweat.

Isabel was still in bed the day our exam results arrived. Geoffrey brought up the envelopes on a silver salver. His shoes creaked outside the door. He gave a slow knock. Isabel was striking matches, one after another, her eyes focused on the flames until they burnt down to her fingers. The burnt match ends creating a kind of chaos across the duvet. The door opened and Geoffrey's torso appeared.

"Hi, girls," he said. We neither lifted our heads nor answered.

"See what I've got for you here." Isabel lit another match. Her face disappeared behind a cloud of smoke then came back into sharp focus through the dissipating scarves of sulphur. A fleeting twitch of anxiety passed across her face like a ghost through a wall. Daddy, with a dewy eye, presented the envelope to Isabel as though it was a head he'd just procured. She laid down the matchbox.

"Open them both," she said to me.

I was not averse to taking orders given the right occasion. There was my name on one envelope and hers on the other: Isabel de Burgh — the rhythm of it sounding like a requiem for the old, decanted classes. I split the lip of the envelope by worming my finger in beneath its gummed flap. Geoffrey had moved over to her bedside as if he knew the contents of the letter. A tissue-thin square of paper inside the envelope revealed that Isabel had failed, triumphantly. I covered my bottom lip with my top lip in a gesture of condolence and said "Poor Isabel", in a voice oddly reminiscent of the coo Phileda reserved for sympathy amongst the villagers.

Geoffrey reached out a hand that had a fresh, burgeoning rash upon it and touched hers, pale. Ascension lurked in my darker regions. Then she did what I least expected. The blood drained from her face and she began to cry. It gave me the gooses. She threw her arms around her father's neck and wailed, "Oh Dad." I leaned back against the windowsill and longed for the microscope an old professor of my mother's acquaintance had promised me years ago.

Never a truer love was witnessed. I marvelled that such a thing was still possible between fathers and daughters of a certain age. He said, "*Shuussh.*" Isabel's prettiness faded during tears; she bore the saturated look of wet sand. It made me think that where there is pity there are enemies. To pity someone was to denounce them as a weakling. I watched with the same furtive fascination as I had once watched horses copulate. The bliss of their embrace overtook them and looking over her shoulder at me he inferred, without uttering a word, that I would never know a love like this. I met his gaze as truthfully as I could. The whole room seemed suddenly cold and colourless, like the inside of an empty fridge. The lavender-reeking drawers and the gleaming mirrors, and my hair, touched by some other electricity in the room, flying up like the plaits of a Dutch puppet; the signs and the edicts, and the snapshots in silver-mounted frames reminding me of not a single summer holiday. It seemed there was malice in everything. Naturally, I got not a word of congratulation for my spectacular straight A success.

There was an old bike of Isabel's in the coach house that still had stabilisers on. I don't know why but an image of its small white wheels, hard and cracked with age, came to me then. For whatever reason they reminded me how bad I'd been at catching balls, and no matter how well you thought you knew someone you could never be exactly sure what was going on inside their heads. How little I knew Isabel. How surprised I'd be in time.

Outside it had begun to rain; the scent of damp, warm gravel flooded the room. Gunshot down the valley. Geoffrey's shoulder was wet with her tears. He stroked her hair. Their affection for each other fired itself into me like the crossed swords on a Meissen teacup. A feeling that had been knocking at the inside of my head since my arrival at Critchley suddenly burst in and splinters flew. I knew what I would do. I would fashion a talisman out of Isabel; I would sand her down until there was nothing left but bone. I made a pact with the soft underside of my hand that Geoffrey de Burgh would know what it was to lose the one thing he loved most in all the world. I would take from them what I had never had.

# CHAPTER
# THREE

Long summer days. The garden full of voluptuous blossoms of a kind I'd never seen before: some tall, thin and bristly, of the toilet brush variety, others that fell apart like confetti when you touched them, as if in anticipation of the potpourri they would soon become.

The borders were full of bright pinpricks of colour. Often I would walk with Phileda in the afternoons, leaving Isabel to her magazines, marooned in love land. Phileda grew to like me even more because I took an interest in her flowers. I understood their language, she said. It wasn't everyone that could. She knelt down to the cabbages and poured sentiment over them like lotion, their green bonneted faces beseeching from the loam, while I grew high on the scent of jasmine and tomatoes cooking on their stalks behind glass, nearly putting my growing pains behind me — almost falling for her strokes, the burrs in her voice, the rings of old gold on her fingers. The cosy little peach-house chats.

"I'd like to travel eventually." No I wouldn't, actually, but it was the kind of easy platitude Phileda liked best. There were things I could have told her that would have shocked her to the core. I wanted her to know me and approve. But there was nothing good I could tell her about myself except what I made up. She asked me about my childhood. I said it was blissful, beautiful: bucolic in the extreme. I invented picnics and ponies and five-barred gates to lean over, and blackberries and bonfires and tadpoles in jars. Anything rather than risk her pity. It was sympathy I feared most; it may have stopped up the hole in my heart and upset everything.

She said, "You must find us very dull after that." I said, on the contrary, there was truth and beauty to be found in all walks of life.

I retied her apron strings in a tighter knot when they broke apart; brushing the fleshy tip of an arum lily with my finger, exclaiming: "How perfect, how beautiful, my favourite!"

"What a darling you are to notice." Discarded croquet mallets on the lawn; the bell metal in its cote, occasionally resounding; the weather vane and its old-boned creak catching on the breeze.

Soon, relatives arrived. An old aunt and an uncle: Geoffrey's brother. She, of the fey, broken type — an arrow snapped in two; he with a funny walk and overshooting jaw — *Homo* sapped and flagging in his light brown tweeds and suede shoes; a pink newspaper trapped beneath his arm, in lieu of a cane. A waft of polished buttons hanging about him.

It was obvious to me that there was rivalry between the two brothers of a kind that had been buried in a grave half filled with broken toy aeroplanes and, latterly, bounced and bailed-out cheques. Reading between the lines: Geoffrey had inherited, Michael had not. It suited me fine: the brooding contention, the semi-hatreds flaring beneath linen napkins, to be doused continually by the pouring of more drink — I felt, given the right moment, that there was a small work of art to be made of it. Right from the off, Phileda clucked and overcompensated, kept bolting off into anecdotes that brought them right back to the meat of the matter — like the time she'd caught her fingers in the car door while collecting Michael from the pub on the afternoon of his mother's funeral. She held up a crooked fingernail that bulged grotesquely beneath red nail varnish. Everyone looked away, including Geoffrey, as though she was showing off the stump of an amputated limb. Isabel muttered "Gross" as she walked across the kitchen, bare feet sticking to the terracotta tiles. I wanted to take the hand as a prince would and kiss the imperfection — honour it. But it was all fruitless. There was not the space in this huge house for the memorable gesture. Only the flippant was acceptable; only that which skimmed the surface.

The following day was my sixteenth birthday. The occasion was made known to the household by the arrival of an ugly card from my mother, former greengrocer's stock by the look of it, and three red roses I knew she couldn't afford. On the card, there was a cartoon boy with long eyelashes embracing a girl in frills, with little hearts fluttering up from their lips. They both wore tartan caps. I wanted to say the card meant nothing to me, but I couldn't bring myself to; the best I could manage was a laugh and Isabel laughed too.

Hurried gifts were rustled up from a stockpile of given gifts — soap with the price tag still on and a locket Isabel had never worn that would remain empty for as long as it belonged to me. Then Phileda said to Isabel, "Darling, you will make an effort tonight, won't you?" She had on a dress that had horse bits and leather straps printed across it.

Isabel gave her a withering look through her fringe and said, "What can you mean?"

"Tonight. You will make yourself presentable, won't you? Change out of your jeans. You know what Aunt Bridget can be like. And it is a special occasion."

Isabel turned to me and said, "Thank God you're here," and turned up the television until it blared. Phileda touched her nose, as though it gave her pain and left the room.

"Come on, Is," I said, snatching the remote control out of her hand while helping myself to the bottom layer of chocolates. An idea was growing in my mind. "Let's dress up tonight."

"Have you caught their disease?" she asked. "Their disease?" she said again, enunciating the two syllables.

I said, "It could be fun, if you wanted it to be. It's called making the most out of a rapidly failing situation. We'll go to the old dress cupboard in the attic and find something that'll really turn their heads." Isabel seemed to be tasting the idea in her mouth, she sucked in her cheeks and bit her lower lip, leaving faint teeth marks. And then her interest suddenly ignited like parched grass and she jumped to her feet.

"OK, but the blue number's mine," and we both ran out of the room, the theme tune from Starsky and Hutch following us up the stairs.

All day we worked on our outfits. The attic was dusty and overly warm, and all over the pale boards flies lay cocooned in cobwebs like babies gauzed in afterbirth. I'd always had a good feeling about attics. (They were places of suppressed feeling, invariably where the servants had lived, gagged by a stronger sense of decorum than those who slept beneath.) The attics of Critchley Hall were composed of a series of small rooms redolent of red fingers and pale faces and someone else's boots that undoubtedly pinched. There were metal-framed beds pushed tightly under the eaves, newspaper fans in the fireplaces and bits of broken china laid out on cardboard. In one of these rooms, an oak wardrobe with an oval mirror in its middle contained the dresses. A breeze of camphor with the opening door revealed a line of dresses hanging side by side, each with an echo of the ballroom clinging to it; striped lines of dusky fabric, the colour of sucked sweets.

Isabel bagged the pale blue dress, claiming she'd always wanted to make an entrance in it. She threw off all her clothes and wriggled into the dress, arms up. She turned to the mirror and announcing herself with a verbal drum roll said, "De, de," throwing her palms out. She stroked the fabric of the dress, lingering over her hips, luxuriating in her own gorgeousness at the slide of her hands. To see her in that dress made me like everything, except her.

Dinner was to be a formal occasion: the first meal eaten in the dining room since my arrival at Critchley Hall. I felt it called for a little glitz and glamour to banish the echo of my childhood years.

"Your turn," she said. "How about this one?" pulling a pink, floaty number out of the wardrobe. "It'll bring out your flesh tones. Come on, strip off." Isabel looked at me in a way that was not entirely becoming. I felt like a land mass upon which her eyes alighted like lost seabirds. I'd seen that look in swimming pools before. I suspected she knew I had problems with nudity, particularly my own. Her glance proffered a dare full of fugitive meaning that I'd have been proud to claim as my own under different circumstances.

Partly because I was intoxicated by the hot spotlight of her attention and partly because to refuse would mean instant humiliation, I began to take off my clothes. She watched, one arm resting on the mantelpiece, a smile playing about her lips. The undressing gave me a warm, overcrowded sensation in the centre of my stomach, as though the seeds of her fascination pierced me with honey-tipped arrows. Out of the corner of my eye, I caught a headline of an advert from an old copy of *Picture Post* which lay open on the bed. It said: IT'S SOUND SLEEP THAT KEEPS NERVES STEADY. I wished only for a Venus shell and a scarf of pale hair. On a bald square of oilcloth, I stood in my underwear that had been washed so many times you couldn't see the size on the label.

"My, my. You are a big girl. That's quite a figure you've got there." It was true I was big for my age. I was two sizes bigger than Isabel. She said, "Wait there," and ran downstairs. I heard her mother's bedroom door open and close. She was back in an instant, clutching a make-up bag the size of a small picnic hamper. "Come and sit in the light," and I obeyed her instruction and moved to the window still in my underwear. She lifted up my chin and said, "Go like that," pouting her lips like an angry monkey. I did as she asked and she painted my lips with small, articulate movements of a soft brush, her face so close to mine I could see the open pores of her skin. I felt the beat of a cottonwool ball against my brow, the flutter of a blusher brush against my cheek and then the gentle snag upwards of the mascara brush as she drew it against my eyelashes. She worked like a sculptor moulding clay, her face fixed in a hard stare of concentration. When she had finished she stepped back to view her work. She smiled.

In the light of the bare bulb, I looked at myself in the oval mirror and felt for the first time a spark of admiration for my own body. Isabel pulled the dress off its hanger and handed it to me. The dress slid on to me. I on to it. I knew then, for the first time, what my body had the power to do. The tight chiffon holding up my breasts like proffered gifts.

"Nice," said Isabel.

To make things better once, my mother recited a poem she said she'd written for me. It went: "I wandered lonely as a cloud . . ." I didn't have the heart to tell her I knew. I just took her hand and squeezed it, and she said, "You like it, don't you?"

56

"Yes, I like it," I said. "When did you learn to write like that?"

"I've always loved books," she said.

We were high up on a mountainside, sitting idly with our backs in the hammock of a wire fence. The larks we could hear but couldn't see. The sheep in peeling fleeces were settling beside the soil banks. I squeezed the sinking sun between my thumb and finger. She was in one of her varying moods, when lies would slip out of her like oiled babies out of fishwives. Her age was especially variable in moods like these; she would tell people she was older than she really was, to allow herself the opportunity for sadness when no one said, "You can't be." But most variable of all was her love of me. She looked to the horizon and said, "Go on, it's your turn to talk."

So I talked, with my head leaning against her breast so that I could hear the echoes of her replies resounding in her ribcage, inventing bad news because I knew it cheered her up. Again and again we came back to the woman who had set light to herself up on the Frith. The woman who had driven to the well-known picnic spot, parked the car, put on the handbrake, checked her make-up in the mirror, poured petrol over herself, then dropped a lighted match into the folds of her green checked skirt. I saw the outline of her face much clearer than that of anyone I knew. There was still a burnt patch in the lay-by where it had happened and it was said that nothing would grow there. Dental records were the only means of identification.

I asked my mother why she thought the woman had bothered to put the handbrake on, but she snapped, "How should I know." And I felt my time in the charmed zone slipping away, with her going cold on me. I flattered myself that I was the maggot stitched inside her flank eating up her canker with relish, in the certain knowledge that, like cabbage, it was doing me good. I started each day thinking I could change things for her; I ended them knowing I could not.

I was thinking of the burnt woman and the handbrake as Isabel and I made our entrance into the dining room — did she push in the release button and pull up the arm smoothly or did it rasp on the metal notches inside its sleeve? We stood behind the double doors hearing the sound of muffled voices within. "Open them," said Isabel, and touched by her excitement, I grasped the handles with both hands and yanked open the doors with more force than was necessary. The voices died. There was a smell of lamb gravy and at the far end of the room ripples in the old glass of the sash windows were distorting the trees outside.

Geoffrey and Phileda sat at the polished table opposite one another, flanked by Bridget and Michael — their faces fixed on us like startled cats confined to a cardboard box. I saw the colour of my flesh in the dome of a silver salver, lips blazing and my hair, stiff with hairspray, piled up like coiled rope on top of my head. Tall wall mirrors showed me the rest of myself in a fleeting glance: I saw myself four times over; the real me barely recognisable beneath the crust of expensive accoutrement, borrowed, unbeknown to Phileda, from her dressing table. Someone had rescued the small gathering of birthday cards from the bedroom floor and removed them to the mantelpiece. My mother's card had been brought to the fore and it faced me where I sat. It wouldn't stand up on account of its damp, curling edges and later it fell from its place amidst the carriage clock and candlesticks, where events overtook it and it lay forgotten in a coal scuttle for weeks afterwards.

We took our places at the table. "Well, well," said Michael. "Growing up in all the right ways, I see." A very pretty blush bled upwards from Isabel's breastbone. Keeping his eyes on me, Geoffrey shook out his napkin so forcibly it cracked like flapping washing.

"You needn't have made quite such an effort, girls," said Phileda.

"Oh, I don't know," said Geoffrey, "the results are rather spectacular, don't you think?" again with his eyes on me. My plan was unfolding in all the right ways.

They started to talk again and the meal got under way. Mostly it was conversation that ridiculed some lesser person. The shop assistant who didn't know what an avocado was. The garage mechanic who'd poured weedkiller on his parents' lawn while they were on holiday, to inhibit growth so he wouldn't have to mow it so often. Michael asking Isabel if she'd like to take the boat out to Bardsey some time. Geoffrey wore a tie that had a little belonging insignia on it just below the knot. The black mark of my caste throbbed invisibly on my forehead. Isabel watched to see if I would use the right cutlery.

I concentrated hard on sliding the cold, green soup into my mouth. Phileda's bangles tinkled each time she raised the spoon to her mouth. Her face was red from the two cocktails Geoffrey had given her before dinner. Above Geoffrey's head was a portrait of an ancestor that looked uncannily like him and on the sideboard were several randomly arranged items of family memorabilia relating to the Boer War. To the left and right of his head, the wall was crammed with smaller paintings. There was one of a child weeping over a dog: the men in waistcoats, the women in bonnets. It had a title with a question mark beneath it. During the course of the evening Phileda tried to be kind by drawing me into the conversation. With my colouring, Bridget asked, did I prefer cashmere or alpaca? I said I preferred Jacob sheep, and thought of the grease that rubbed off on your hands from wrapping fleeces. Her skin was creased like paper smoothed out after origami. Isabel was making a sea urchin out of a spot of water on the table with the tip of her fork, having half a conversation with her mother.

"What do you know about Pompeii?"

"Quite a lot as it happens."

This diversion in the conversation appeared to herald the end of the evening. I was thinking how my mother would laugh at this kind of talk. She, too, ridiculed everything except animals and the law. She held judges in high esteem. Michael, who was very drunk, began to get to his feet. A sailor in the same predicament would have stayed on the quayside until morning, aiming his profanities at the seagulls. Geoffrey raised his glass to me. Bridget, with a hairgrip showing, was pronouncing upon the iniquities of bought cake. I knew that if I pushed up the window and dangled my hand into the night my fingers would come up black.

A row got up from nowhere, like a wind at sea. "But the rabbit was in pain," Isabel was suddenly shouting at her mother. "It was dying there in front of me on the path, with its eyes popping out of its head. The country is cruel and I'm going to leave here and move to the city as soon as I can." Phileda told her to stop overreacting and that myxomatosis had done the farmers a great favour in the 1950s.

I was thinking of a cold Sunday afternoon and how a vicar must feel turning himself out to deliver a sermon no one would hear. "That's what you really think, isn't it?" Isabel was shouting. "That's what you really think." There was a staccato shush of heavy chairs being drawn backwards across rucked-up carpet; everyone getting to their feet; a confusion of slammed doors. Possibly tears. The dining room was suddenly deserted. I finished my own raspberry parfait and Isabel's too, feeling the cold knobs of ice disintegrating on the saucer of my tongue, then I rose from my chair and went to look for Geoffrey. I knew he'd be waiting.

The passageway was dark. I walked past the cloakroom. Michael was urinating into the washbasin. The taps were full on; the dim little room smelling like the inside of a wellington boot. Geoffrey was standing on the outside step. He was smoking a thin cigar, tapping his thigh with his long fingers — so different from the boy whose golden hair his mother had made promises over: a different laugh, a different nose after the first had been damaged by a fall from a pony with a wall eye. Phileda had told me. I joined him on the wide step.

He said, "Did you know the reason we dream is to let our fears out? And if we didn't dream, we'd go mad." After that the rest came easily. Men were there to be used; I'd learned that from my mother but sometimes, as in her case, it backfired. It wouldn't in mine.

No, I didn't know, I said. Before I did anything important I always looked for strange things happening in the sky. That night there was an oddish red glow behind the trees. I guessed it was the lights of the nearest city. I took it as a portent, a sign that every quiver of the human heart was preordained. There was a flapping in the trees as of a large bird falling off a branch. I scanned the inside of my mind for a reason why I should not do this and finding none I reached out and took Geoffrey's hand, and drew him silently towards the darkness; towards the end of his life as he had known it.

The garage doors were open. Along the far wall there was a wooden bench strewn with tools. Geoffrey directed me towards the big old Rolls and said, "Get in." There was sand on the floor soaking up oil spills. I had to pick up the train of my dress to step up onto the running board of the car. It dignified the moment to the point where I nearly gave in and ran away. But his big frame was coming in behind me, barring the way, and I heard the solid clunk of the door closing. He covered me like a black cloud. His breath, his leaden eyelids swamping me in darkness.

The smell of the leather upholstery reminded me of a journey I'd taken in my mother's car a long time ago; she wrapped in her fake fur, surrounded by fourteen volumes of the *Encyclopaedia Britannica*, her only possessions. She'd said, "If anyone's doing the leaving, it'll be me this time." The engine started; bare legs glued to the hot upholstery. I'd been given a pacifying drink to suck up through a striped straw, bright orange and warm; spilt crisps already gritty behind my knees.

The memory extinguished in a blink with the second touch of his hand and I was back there in real time on a threshold strewn with newly plucked flowers.

From out of the back of the car, my eyes traced over and over the green letters of a sign for Castrol Oil. He pushed up my dress and his hand felt like a small silken pet, exploring and sliding between my legs, trying to find its way in. The pink chiffon tore. It was old and gauzy and the dust from it made me sneeze. At the touch of his hand I felt I had a velvet core and liquid was pouring from me. It was the coldest and the warmest thing I'd ever known. Perhaps I would be brave and only half remember this night. He began to fumble with his zip. There was a sound of everything giving way. I didn't want it to go any further but I knew it had to. My sacrifice was incomplete.

A raspberry seed from the evening's dessert nudged between my teeth. I focused on the shape of the summer bats flying in a figure of eight outside the window. I had to brace myself like a piece of iron against the car door for the haft and the shaft of the thickening muscle. There was a fusing sensation in me, a feeling of being forced through the strings of a tennis racket. I felt myself loom large above him, as if I was a near-death experience from which he would never wake. He mumbled words of Catholic smut into my shoulder, thinking I was his mother, his rabbit, his chiselled child. The way I did it was by playing down the nature of the experience; it was a comma, merely a comma, and the fancy dress I had on proved it.

Dry tears trickled nevertheless. Had I caught them in a silver dish they might have nourished the world with their wisdom. The things I knew; the lessons I had learned along the way. This was a new lesson, a new experience, but it left me feeling empty, a tree trunk hollowed out. I sneezed again, this time at the yeasty smell of him. It was only at the moment when he pulled away that I began to feel like an inferior cut of meat. And that was it. The taking against an iron will. It was my will that took. It carried me in a blanket almost to the afterlife.

There was a blank moment when I just lay back imagining what I must have looked like from above, filling up the corner of the car with my dress, a ragged frill above my waist. His words now burbling, for the record, aiming at the salving of conscience, "Oh God, no, what have I done?" and the like, reminding me of precisely what I had managed to achieve in thirteen and a half minutes; and the tiny confirming whimperings that was the sound of his future fragmenting. He pushed himself up and out of the car. A coldness spread through my bones as though the raspberry parfait was reforming itself to ice inside me. I was suddenly confronted with an overwhelming desire for a boiled egg of my mother's making, with strips of buttered bread moving out from the edge of the plate like the sun's white-hot rays. It was the only thought in the world that gave me any comfort. And the quilt. I wished too for my mother's quilt with the smell of cooked breakfasts contained within its folds.

I played with the tools on the wooden bench for a little while afterwards. There was an old-fashioned drill. It bit into the worktop when I turned the handle and left a small dent of white wood, very obvious and new, amidst the coating of oil spills and dark stains. There was a hacksaw too and a plane. I ran it over the edge of the bench and a thin curl of wood rose from its mouth like a sea horse. Outside, beyond these walls, were all the places I had known during my childhood: the palsied spinneys and the darkening copses; places I had tired of, grown restless in; the old quarry I had roamed in, where I had scratched messages of dull despair onto stones with fossils on their backs. Seeking always for a different fate: I would not get my arm trapped in a baling machine; I would not emigrate to Canada and sing sad songs in bars with heel-pocked floors. No, my fate would be distinct.

When I arrived back at the house, all the lights were blazing and the front door stood open. The smell of autumn was in the air. The leaves of the lime trees were already beginning to float down to the ground, brown.

Isabel came running from the house like an avenging angel, with the tails of her dress billowing outwards. "Where've you been. What's happened? Dad's in a terrible state. What's happened?" she asked again, casting an eye over my torn dress. There was nothing for it but to tear the meat from the bone. I put my hands over my face and feigned tears. Her perfect, milk-pale brow puckered into folds. "What are you telling me?" she asked, almost tenderly. Her hands were on my shoulders now. Her face like a mirror reflecting my dishevelment. For dramatic effect I kept silent as long as I could, as long as the moment would stretch. But Isabel demanded; kept asking what in the hell had happened, what perfidy, in so many words, had befallen me. I began to formulate a speech on my tongue, but try as I might I could not make the words spill out of my mouth.

The porch light flickered. There was gravel needing to be swept off the top step. A tangible grief swept over Isabel's features as she comprehended the meaning of my silence. Her eyes willed me to contradict her. But I could not. She took off her mother's paisley wrap and placed it round my shoulders. She said: "God help us", and I almost spurted a laugh at the sound of the semi-child with the mock solemn words of an adult in her mouth.

There were angry sounds coming from the house, of people moving around the rooms with conviction. There was also music from the record player, Fauré's

*Pelléas et Mélisande*, which I guessed Michael had put on. I was amazed at how much the human heart could absorb in one go. The hallway looked smaller somehow; it reminded me suddenly of the lobby of a cheap hotel on account of the onyx cigarette lighter and shiny, reproduction andirons lying next to the fireplace. Phileda's jigsaw lay almost finished on the open flap of the bureau. I hadn't inspected it closely before. It was an image of Isabel as a child, in some place in the garden, wearing a thick yellow pullover, standing like a soldier with her hands flat against her thighs and a yellow dog at her side with its tongue lolling out. She had a tiny white flower tucked behind her ear. A dog rose — or something of that kind — with the thorns picked off. As luck would have it, I caught the tray with my hip as I brushed past and the pieces spilled to the ground; pieces of Isabel fragmenting: a hand, an arm, part of a foot that also contained the leg of a garden table in the foreground. I stooped to gather them up but Isabel was at my side saying, "Sod the jigsaw." I pretended to cry again and my knees were shaking, though not involuntarily this time.

I ran up to the green bathroom and locked the door. I knew it was a dangerous time and that my thoughts needed nursing. I ran a bath and took off my clothes and looked at myself in the mirror. My back and thighs were criss-crossed with the pattern of the car's leather upholstery: a body contained within red bars. I felt the wound between my legs would never heal.

The sound of raised voices downstairs went on long into the night. Words floated up to me like cooking smells: "brutal", "alternative", "wicked", "she's only a child", amongst other snatches. I slept on top of the bed. When I woke in the early hours I found someone had covered me over with a duvet.

When I came down the following morning Phileda was sitting at the kitchen table behind a wall of breakfast cereal. The aunt and uncle had already left. I knew she was waiting for me. Her cheeks were streaked with tears. She looked up and straightaway said, "Whatever happened last night, I will find a way to make it up to you, Diane." It was the first time she had ever used my name. She got up and crossed the room; clasped me in her arms, our bodies like hands in prayer, straight and sensitive: an imperceptible suction. My chin rested on her shoulder, so I could feel her bones and imagine the blood in her veins coursing through her body like car headlights in a country lane.

I told her not to worry; said that in my opinion rape was not the worst thing that could happen to a girl. When I said that, I began to wonder who was consoling who, for she made a sound one would normally associate with the slaughter of young turkeys. Lack of love mattered more, I told her. Her grip tightened. It was more of a light squeeze, as if all her strength had leaked out and lay shining and glittering in a pool at her feet. I kept my eyes focused on the view of the garden through the window. There were banks of leaves beneath the trees and places where the beech mast lay scattered across the graves of three pet dogs. The fountain was covered by a net; the garden forks all rinsed and hanging in the shed.

I looked up and saw Isabel leaning with her head against the doorframe, looking so helplessly sad I thought it was a double bluff. I wanted to ask her what the French word for monkey was — just so I could hear her say it and because I knew it made her laugh. But her features remained tucked in like a bed with hospital corners. It was no double bluff. Geoffrey had already left the house.

If I have one overriding image of Isabel from our teenage years, it is of her that morning after Geoffrey had left, leaning against the doorframe with her childhood heights notched into its scuffed paintwork. Her mascara had run and she still had on the blue dress from the night before — "the frigging blue dress" as she later called it, thinking it somehow responsible for all the ills of the evening. "Blue is an unlucky colour for me," she said, "strange how vanity makes you forget stuff."

I was sitting at the table opposite Phileda. Isabel came over and put her arms round my neck and kissed the top of my head; a light kiss: her lips bouncing against my hair like an insect alighting on a sour bloom. I had never seen such concern on another's face before. I could see how sympathy could become a drug to the poor of mind and why after a visit to the hospital my mother always said there were some people who didn't want to get better.

The day Isabel died, she also wore blue. Perhaps she had forgotten her previous superstition relating to the colour; or perhaps it was just vanity again.

# CHAPTER
# FOUR

It emerged that Geoffrey had been unfaithful twice
before. It was all grist to the red rag of Phileda's
menopause. "Once more and you're out," she'd told
him some years earlier. I was the third strike. No one
thought to accuse me, a child, as Phileda had so
erroneously put it. I was blameless: a starched napkin
that nothing could despoil. He didn't come back for his
belongings. She had them sent. There were no
protestations. I assisted with the packing. "Come and
help me," she said, "it might even release something in
you." To release anything further, I knew, would have
been to excite tempests; to have uprooted trees; to have
torn the roofs off buildings. We went into Geoffrey's
study. It was dark even with the light on and smelt
faintly of whisky and Turkish spices: a room where a
large maned animal would retire to chew bones. It was
book-lined for show; bare boards, a putter behind the
door.

We didn't pack so much as tip. Three tea chests,
open-mouthed and begging for the contents of the big,
leather-topped desk. Dovetailed drawers revealed an
assortment of watch straps: some striped, some leather,
always the bottom strap; there were tablet packets and

buttons but nothing incriminating, as if a chapel-goer had sorted through it in case of sudden death. There were some things I might have purloined had Phileda not been watching: a sheath with ties to protect a damaged finger and a miniature toothbrush to clean the innards of a clock. We worked industriously and mostly in silence. Phileda hummed but I couldn't tell what tune. By the afternoon every last pen top and striped shirt Geoffrey had ever owned had gone from the house. The furniture would remain she said; if he wanted it, he'd have to fight her through the courts. If he pursued a claim she'd take him to the cleaners. She said he wouldn't; negative publicity meant dishonour to a family like his and he was lucky he wasn't facing a rape charge.

"Phileda, if you wanted me to, I'd testify in court," I said.

"I know you would, my dear, but it wouldn't go that far." Geoffrey was a coward. He'd make do with a flat on the Edgware Road and would return to the sleezy, easy life he'd had when she'd first met him.

Isabel stayed in her room. She said she was committing her thoughts to paper; that writing was "cathartic", the best possible cure for a lost father. But the word cathartic too closely resembled the word catheter for me to approach it with any kind of seriousness; it smacked of substance being drawn out under duress by use of pumps and pulleys. I took her a cheese and chutney sandwich and a glass of cold milk, folding a paper napkin into a bird as I'd been taught when I'd worked out of sight in the kitchen of the village local. But she cast the tray to the bedside table without comment and said, "You don't have to be so brave, you know." I said I held cowardice in fairly low esteem.

"It's quite natural to feel angry."

"But I'm not angry."

"You have to be."

"I'm not," I said, watching her tug at the skin around a painted toenail. We paused while she induced a satisfactory spurt of blood from the side of the nail and then dabbed at it with a scrap of tissue she'd procured especially for the purpose.

"Then what would it take to make you angry?"

I suddenly wanted to discuss everything with her. I wanted to tell her of the occasions my stepbrother would sit astride my stomach while pinning my arms down with his knees. How, as I lay incapacitated with rage on the living-room floor of The Shack on the Lower Road, I took comfort from the smell of the dirt in the carpet and the sight of the chewing gum stalactites stuck to the underside of the slate mantelpiece. His game was to dribble a string of spit over my face, to let it hang like a bead from a rosary above my mouth, before sucking it back up to his lips. Once, a moment too late in the sucking, it fell onto my face. It ran like a tear down the side of my nose. It was black spit too, on account of the liquorice shoelaces he'd recently devoured. Anger was a luxury I could not afford.

"Go on, what would it take?"

But Isabel had no appetite for such reminiscences. She bored as easily as she wept.

"How would I know," I said. "How can anyone tell until it actually happens." What she really wanted was to talk about herself, so I said, "What about you?"

She pulled her feet onto her thighs and began to tell me of an incident involving a boy she'd met last summer on a yachting holiday in the southern Mediterranean; an incident so marginally disreputable I thought she'd made it up. He'd stolen her diary one evening while both their families were dining companionably in the back room of a local restaurant. The walls, she remembered, were hung with fishing nets studded with pink shells. She'd got to know him over the few days they had spent playing boules on the quayside. Being the children of wealthy parents they recognised something of themselves in each other and friendship seemed only a matter of being together. She said the place must have cast a spell on her; it was very hot and there was talk of voodoo in the hills that involved the ritual slaughter of young goats and hares. She liked the boy and she thought he liked her; but then the diary had gone missing out of her straw bag that hung from the back of her chair in the restaurant and she knew he'd taken it.

The next day paper aeroplanes began to rain down on the deck of the yacht. They were pages torn from her diary and they emanated from the boat in the next berth; pages upon which she had confessed her fondness for him. His face appeared to her expressionless as he stood on the deck throwing out her most secret words, as though they were javelins sent to wound her. Messages with bent wings and crumpled noses were found in the yacht's sails for days afterwards. Only later did she feel angry, as angry as she had ever felt before in her life. But the anger she felt towards him was nothing in comparison to the anger she now felt towards her father and what he had done to me. This new anger left her feeling cold inside she confessed, not hot, as with the boy.

Hoping I would repay the confidence with a confidence, she paused and looked at me with the face of one who has been told from a young age that she is beautiful — i.e. expectantly. Her nails, I noticed, were soft and pitiful like a foal's hooves newly out of the womb. I guessed she wanted to know what sex with her father had been like. I'd heard of Russian women eating their own placentas after birth and this carried with it something of the same unwholesome aura; far more dark and dangerous than the actual act with him had been. So I began to talk, slowly at first, not wishing to give too much away, not wishing to lessen the experience in her eyes. It was murky business indeed. There were bitter grinds floating in it.

His lust was brief and greedy, I said, sharp, stabbing, like having a starfish wash in and out of you, or glass. "Go on," she said, her eyes wide and black like sequins sewn into a wedding dress. I spoke of violations, immolations, and how when I asked him to desist, he swore, blue, hard. It was easy once I got going. I'd learned a lot about the art of lying from my mother because she was no good at it. I had perfected the craft that she had sown in me. Isabel swallowed the whole thing, right down to the last momentary loss of consciousness. When I came to, there were more tears pouring down her face.

"I loved him," she said, between shuddering gulps of breath. "I really loved him."

"But you can go on loving him," I said.

"What? After all that? It's hard to feel affection for a pervert," she said.

"Love doesn't just stop because someone does something bad."

"It does for me," she said. But it didn't. Even I knew that. I, who had never loved anyone in the right way, knew that real love lay somewhere beyond death, and that a bad deed was no barrier to it.

A few days later Phileda ordered us out of the house to get some fresh air. Over the previous week Isabel had not left the house. She had made only short trips to the kitchen from her bedroom to make strawberry-meal drinks for herself or to see whether her stuff from the catalogue had arrived. She liked to run down and get the packages before Phileda saw them. Sometimes she wouldn't even bother to open them; she would put them straight under her bed, unopened. She said she liked the thought of a stockpile of waiting presents. They gave her something to look forward to.

Phileda suggested we take the ponies out. "Horses," said Isabel. "Anything over fourteen hands high is a horse, not a pony."

"Horses," said Phileda vaguely. "Yes. Horses," as if she had forgotten what they were. It was the first time

I'd seen her without lipstick or make-up. Her face looked brittle and pale, like a knuckle sucked clean and laid on the side of a dinner plate.

Surprising us both, Isabel seized on the idea and went off to get changed. Every activity required a change of clothes, as if her life was a play that demanded frequent changes of costume. It was not a good day for a ride. I'd forgotten how depressing that first plunge into the chill could be, like climbing into a bath of second-hand water on a Sunday night with the prospect of homework still to come. The afternoon was resolutely dull. The sky seemed grey and pointless without the sun to animate it. And the trees, too, looked thin and sparse as if they were gaining no nourishment at all from the soil, which was said by the village gossip to contain the bodies of several dead druids. Perhaps it was my early life amongst the turnip-tops that had put me off the idea of fresh air, like the reformed smoker who can no longer stand the smell of cigarettes.

We went through to the stable yard. I looked over towards the garage and saw that the door of the old Rolls was still open as Geoffrey had left it on that fateful night. Isabel saw me looking and ran over and slammed the garage doors closed. I resolved to go back later in case there was anything to see. For the same reason that I found it necessary to look in my handkerchief after blowing my nose.

Isabel was wearing jodhpurs. I allowed her the hacking jacket too, but laughed until the tears rolled down my cheeks when I saw she was wearing a hairnet.

She put her hand to it and it sprang off her head like a frightened animal. I laughed even harder when I saw her stooping to snatch it off the ground. It made me feel brave and reckless like I knew everything and she knew nothing, and even with her start in life she still looked stupid picking a hairnet off the ground. But then I remembered I was wearing her old jeans and a pair of Phileda's wellingtons, or gumboots as she insisted on calling them. And suddenly the hairnet wasn't funny any more. Isabel had given me the run of her wardrobe but I didn't much care for her taste in clothes. Everything was adorned, swirled, encrusted with some mollusc-like pattern. I preferred plain: black, blue or green, in that order. That morning I had chosen an angora sweater because I knew I'd stretch it and she wouldn't be able to wear it again. Isabel, in her churchy way, had given it to me gladly.

There was nothing I wanted less than to be out in the cold. I wanted to be back by the Aga making drop scones and writing silly words on the fridge door with the magnetic letters, and grinding coffee beans because I loved the smell and the noise the straining motor made. I didn't want to be out here with the prospect of rain coming on and the clouds gathering and the trees bending their backs. I said so to Isabel. But she had that determined look on her face that dogs have when they're on the lead and have caught the scent of some minxy animal. It annoyed me too that the clock above the stable arch had stopped at ten to three. I felt conspired against. I broke the feeling down into two parts: one half was that Isabel was a good rider; the other was that I couldn't cheat at riding and soon she would see this. I was relying on Isabel to award me the lesser mount so that I could later lay the blame at old dobbin's door.

Sure enough, when we reached the field, she cast her hand towards the smaller, fatter, hairier of the two beasts, the one she called Hester. Tall, black, handsome Darius she kept for herself. We bridled and saddled. I flicked and picked at the ladybirds on Hester's coat, only to find they were fleabites. I liked to be near horses but not necessarily astride them. I liked their companionable warmth and the way they tolerated humans that had nothing to do with bits and whips but everything to do with forgiveness. They forgave you all the time you were on their backs.

The horses reminded me of the feeling next door's garden had given me as a child. Next door was a field and a lane away from The Shack on the Lower Road. Whenever my mother said, "Go where I can't see you," I went to the garden. The back gate was a rusted bedstead you had to climb over. An old lady lived there who kept cats. The garden was very overgrown. Sometimes I'd see her staring out of an upstairs window at me. She never came out or told me to go away, so I kept going back. I became very bold and would drag a broken deckchair out of the shed and sit in the middle of the overgrown lawn, reading, balanced on a thong of torn fabric. I hoped she would come and talk to me. Old box hedges that had once edged the slippery paths had since grown into small, irrelevant trees. Everything was beautiful because man had not interfered, probed or beaten back for a long time. Only the things that had blown over from our farm were ugly: baling twine and torn fertiliser bags, and sometimes lambs' tails that the foxes brought over at night.

Isabel was holding Hester for me and was telling me to get on. I lost the feeling of the garden once I was up in the saddle. It was a long time since I'd been on a horse and had had the experience of sitting astride an ocean, riding the sea waves or a mountain on the move. Isabel alighted like an autumn leaf on Darius's back. She rode like a textbook diagram, with her heels well down in the stirrups and her shoulders pinned back as though to a board. The horses' hooves, in the tunnel of trees that edged the drive, sounded less like hooves and more like the imitation people made with coconuts in nativity plays to indicate the flight from Egypt. It started to rain. My ears wouldn't tuck under the riding hat; they stuck out, flattened by the rim of the hat like the ears of an angry cat. We turned out of the gates. The nice thing about being on a horse was that you could see over hedges into people's living rooms. I liked that. You could see the blue light from the televisions filling up the front rooms and people moving in and out with cups of tea and plates of toast. It reminded me of those nature programmes when they put the camera inside nest boxes. You could tell a lot about people by looking in their front rooms; more than I wanted to know about anyone. And I felt bigger than all of them put together because of the new turn my life had taken and because

I would never be like them. I would never do normal things in front rooms.

The telephone box looked extra red beneath its shining skin of new rain. There were little rivulets of water forming by the sides of the lane. The clouds were low and dark. I kept my fingers entwined in Hester's mane for safety's sake. A bead of cold rain trickled down my neck as we turned off the lane and onto a bridle path.

The worst part of the ride came when Isabel gave me a lesson in posture: "Sit up straight, darling," she said, imitating her mother. But Hester would keep snatching at the verge-side grass, dragging me forward over the pommel of the saddle. "Pull her up, pull her up." I ignored her; tried to imagine birdsong while Hester braced her neck like a crane and continued to bite at the grass. Then I threw my leg over the saddle and slipped to the ground. "Spoilsport," Isabel said. "I need a run, d'you mind?"

"Did somebody speak?" I said, cupping my hand sarcastically behind my ear, but Isabel was already turning into the wind, the bit pulling up Darius's lips to reveal teeth that were stained by the rheum of the field. She squeezed his mudded flank and he moved forward in a bound. It seemed a miraculous movement, as if one of the horses on St Mark's in Venice, had suddenly sprung to life.

Hester had lost interest in the verge and was now wondering where the others had gone. I used a tree stump to launch myself onto her back. I was too big for her. I wanted to get off and lead her all the way up the hill, but the gate was a long way off. Instead we went slowly, picking our way round clods of earth and wayward bracken. When we caught up, Isabel was making a big show of trying to untie the gate from Darius's back. It was a pony-club manoeuvre she insisted, something she had spent a long time practising. Beyond the gate, the damp hedgerows hung over the lane like a crowd behind barricades dropping drips and hips, in place of rubbish. There was a smell of cow manure in the air; they spread it on the fields when the weather was cold so that the thaw would draw it deeper into the earth.

A car pulled up just as Isabel had managed to untie the gate. It had two aerials: one on the back, one on the front, and it moved at a sinister pace like a funeral car. It stopped and a man got out. Then a funny thing happened. The man walked towards us and pulled open the flaps of his beige mac. The day was not quite in focus because of the rain and at first I thought he was wearing beige clothes underneath. But why, I wondered, did the man have a dark triangle painted on the crotch of his trousers? Was it one of those joke aprons husbands wore when they were forced to cook? The ones with the naked body of a woman printed on them.

The man kept his hands in the pockets of his open mac, his knees were bent slightly, as though preparing to jump from the top of a tall building. I heard, in the hilltop silence, his breaths coming faster and faster. I laugh now at my simple-mindedness and how when I realised what he was — a flasher, a mackintosh, a sad drab in an unbelted coat — I was sad for myself because there had been a time of innocence; a time when the fleece of my mind had been white.

Meanwhile, Isabel, by the gate, was gathering herself up to do something rash; something really unlike Isabel. The guileless way she was using her body was a prelim to an outburst of some sort. She pulled her whip out of the right leg of her boot, dug her spurs into Darius's flank and launched herself at the man; so much quick movement it was like a bazaar. "You bastard, you filthy lying bastard," she shouted, while taking a polo crack at his blond legs. This was Isabel straight out of the tube and not even a mirror for miles around, no camera, not even a pond to gaze into. The surprise of it made me smile. "Kill him, kill him," I heard myself whisper, just for the rapture, the sheer excitement of it.

He reached the car; she bore down on him again, bringing her whip hard across his head. "You filthy lying bastard." And then suddenly her reaction made sense. All men were her father; he was the template round which the scissors had cut. A look of bewilderment passed over the man's face, the like of which I had not seen since I pulled a dummy from a baby's mouth. He got into the car and slammed the door. Blood rolled down the side of his head. He reversed the car blindly, but not before Isabel had smashed a wing mirror and drawn her spurred heel across the bonnet. The car sped off down the lane with Isabel in cold pursuit. I could hear Darius's shoes hammering the tarmac. Then silence, with nothing but the birds wheeling in the bruised sky for company.

Hester dropped her head to the verge again and began to crop the grass. I don't know how long I sat there. The rain had stopped and the rough-haired hilltop begged for a smoothing hand. I wanted to touch it, to stroke it, to console something larger than myself. Isabel's fury had surprised me. It was honest, it was shocking, but it was worthy of the highest respect. It had grazed the surface of my need to do her damage; it had almost come too close. Something like pain entered me: not pain of the piercing variety, but pain inflamed, an engorged organ.

I began to laugh. I laughed because I couldn't cry. Tears had never been my forte. I laughed until I thought I would burst; until I did burst and my bladder reneged on me. My body would have its liquid release. The saddle was the loser: the zebra streaks were testimony. I felt no shame, only a strong desire to hide the evidence from Isabel.

On the way back I swabbed the leather seat with dock leaves. Then it began to rain again and soon my misdemeanour became indistinguishable from the wetness of the clouds.

# CHAPTER
# FIVE

Christmas. There was no snow, which was a disappointment to Isabel. The roses flowered prematurely against the peach-house wall: tight, sickly blooms deformed by an early birth. Phileda was anxious. It was unusually mild for the time of year. There was moss in the lawn and mildew staining the windowsills. The swallows' nests were empty, cupped to the underside of the eaves like evicted squats. Winter. A season after my own heart: the season of least expectation. The dark nights prohibited activity. Winter the dark, the cruel; summer the fair, the soft. The house was full of sleeping butterflies that came alive when the heating came on.

Mrs Dawson, the housekeeper and cook of twenty-two years, had been "let go" by Phileda like a creature released back into the wild. I missed the dismissal: half suspected that Phileda had crammed her into a cat basket and driven her miles away from the house before opening the flap. Phileda claimed that without Geoffrey Mrs Dawson was surplus to requirements. For the foreseeable future there would be no more parties at Critchley Hall. There would be no more bubbles, petits fours, glacé cherries and suggestive talk from short men in tartan trousers. The tinkle of champagne glasses would be a thing of the past. She said that from now on she only had eyes for her garden; she would find salvation in the veneration of her vines.

I was glad Mrs Dawson had gone. She came from stock that didn't feel the cold and wore T-shirts all year round. The undersides of her upper arms were pink and pimpled. She was full of common sense — that is the sense of the common: peasant sayings and country lore. I knew she suspected me, but of what I couldn't be sure. It was something in the way she put plates and teacups down before me: with a flourish and no reverence, unlike Isabel whose meals were presented as gifts in the way of frankincense and myrrh.

There was only one small incident that could have fuelled her suspicion. It was the time she caught me leafing through the post on the floor of the porch. As I did every morning, I was checking to see if Geoffrey had written to Phileda. But this time Mrs Dawson came in five minutes early. She'd missed the bus and her son had given her a lift in. She wore trainers because of her bunions and moved silently about the house. That was another thing I disliked about her. I was inspecting the handwriting on an envelope when I heard someone behind me. I looked up and there she was leaning against the doorframe, her little cormorant's eyes, magnified behind heavy lenses, fixed on me. The great savannah of her bosom rested on tightly crossed arms; it rose and fell in silent disapproval of me. I got to my feet and said, "I'm expecting a letter." But I knew she didn't believe me. Girls like me didn't receive letters. She began to watch me after that. Under her gaze I felt like a needle she kept trying to thread.

Gradually, I encouraged Phileda to get rid of her. I highlighted the unnecessary expense, offered to do the cooking myself. And Phileda, in return, was touched by my consideration of her affairs. When Mrs Dawson finally did leave, the house seemed overly large and silent for a time, like a deserted galleon left to roam the high seas.

Neither Phileda nor Isabel knew how to cook. Sad to say, the kitchen was my natural domain. I found there was special enjoyment to be gained from having the right ingredients, unlike The Shack on the Lower Road, where old Cheddar with the green bits cut off made do for Parmesan; turkey for chicken. At Critchley Hall I poured over recipe books in the mornings and planned the evening meal. I watched cookery programmes in the afternoons. I loved the patter: the coat-with-flour, take-two-handfuls spiel; the perfect results again and again.

I chose the moment for telling Isabel and Phileda I would be going home for Christmas with care. We were in the kitchen, Isabel sitting at the faux-oak counter on a high stool, drawing a teaspoon of peanut butter in and out of her mouth. A chef's hat of a soufflé steamed before us. I had no intention of going home for Christmas. Phileda had just come into the kitchen, immaculate, except for a shocking clash of cerise and stool-brown between skirt and scarf — an error of taste.

"Urgh," said Isabel, feigning fright when she saw her mother's clothes. I stamped out the flames of

86

impending ruction by announcing my imminent departure. They both turned and stared at me.

"But it's all settled," said Isabel, a look of shellacked indignation on her face. "You're staying here for Christmas. We can't do without you."

"But Christmas is a family thing," I said.

"Oh yeah, a family thing?" snorted Isabel. "Tell her, Mum, we need her to stay."

As luck would have it, Josy the cat came in and wound itself round Phileda's legs. Most of Phileda's recommendations came through the cat: Josy thinks we should watch television now; Josy thinks the cop did it, etc. The ways of the nursery hung about her like seaweed on a drowned corpse. Phileda snatched her up and held her close to her face. I'd made a pal of Josy and Phileda knew it. I knew how to manipulate a cat's affections. The dispensing of discreet smoked salmon titbits meant that Josy would do things for me she wouldn't do for them. It was the motivating factor in Phileda's regard for me.

She put her ear to the cat's mouth and said, "Josy wants you to stay. Don't you, puss?" The cat threw her a pitying look.

Isabel jumped off the stool. "Well, that's settled then," she said in a feigned Jean Brodie accent. "If Josy says it, that's it. We'll have no more talk of you going home, young lady."

Home is where the heart is. Home is heaven. "Ever let the fancy roam, pleasure never is at home." My memories of Christmas were shop-soiled; they had buttons missing and the zips didn't work. One Christmas for example: tiny white feathers dancing in the sugar bowl, blown in from the turkey plucking. Feathers in the yard, banked in drifts beneath cars. Feathers in beef sandwiches. Sheepdogs licking on a soup of discarded entrails on the shed floor. Paper napkins. A quilted dressing gown. A joke — of a kind not meant to make you laugh — was the thing the pluckers did with the sawn-off turkey legs, pulling on the tendons to make the feet open and close.

My stepsisters and I saw UFOs from our bedroom window one Christmas Eve: five of them, flying up from behind the trees; darting, spherical objects whose brightness left blue trails in the sky. The wild geese that settled on the skirts of our pond after dark, panicked at the night so unexpectedly turned into day. It was like an eclipse the wrong way round in the way it unnerved the birds and animals. The earth was a drum for the heels and hooves of running beasts. The geese got up and I felt the breeze from their wings fan my cheeks as they flew past the open window. Beside me, a stepsister in a floral nightdress began to whimper with the fright of it. The inside of our bedroom was bright with white light as though an angel had come amongst us.

Next door, the voices grew louder. Christmas was the one time of year my mother found her courage. The voices swelled to shouts. There was a thud as of a large piece of furniture falling forward onto something soft. Silence. She called out my name. I tried to unhear it; concentrated on the moving lights, the little suns that moved around the sky with astonishing speed. But the pull of her voice was stronger than the spectacle of the lights. I ran next door and pushed open the door just in time to see the bottle raised above my stepfather's head. His brown trousers were folded neatly over the arm of the chair; the imprint of his knees just visible in them. Her call had been for an audience: lights, curtain, music. Sure that I was watching, she brought the bottle down on his head with the strength of the insane. He fell forward, rucking the counterpane like a seal moving across sand. The one thing I find myself incapable of now is violence. I could no more crush a fly between my fingertips than I could sever my own finger with a blunt knife.

In the morning I told my mother about the spaceships of the night before. She got into a rage and said it was about time I stopped looking for things to be admired for. She said, "Smell that instead," and handed me a bundle of fivers she'd stolen from his back pocket some time during the mélèe. "That's not make-believe." The money smelt of fired shotgun cartridges. It smelt dangerous.

My stepfather took his Christmas meals in the barn sitting on a bale of hay, his big moon face crowned by a paper hat. We took it in turns to deliver cold plates of bacon sandwiches to him. He stayed silent for four days. The bottle had been plastic and only his pride had been injured. Our Christmas stockings, each containing three pieces of fruit, lay forgotten until Boxing Day on the slate slab in the pantry.

I couldn't get the spaceships out of my mind; their eerie, silent presence stayed with me for days afterwards. Their brightness had branded my eyeballs. I saw the imprint of a flying saucer each time I blinked.

"Calling Planet Earth. Anyone at home," Isabel's voice called out to me across the years. Christmas dinner in all its tinselled splendour was laid out before me. The relief of finding myself at a polished table was immense. I smiled at Isabel, almost gratefully. I was minded never to talk about my upbringing to Isabel even though I knew she was curious about it. People got the wrong impression if you felt sorry for yourself and talked about it. In the old days, rich people did good things for the poor so they would look better in the eyes of their peers. Perhaps some thread of DNA in Isabel reminded her of her philanthropic duty to the less well off. She could no longer wander around the bruised and barren countryside doling out bread from a wicker basket as her ancestors had done, but she could take in a social inferior and see whether she could make something of her. But if I was Isabel's social experiment, then she was more so mine. She had already learned in a short time what it was to have a father walk out of her life.

"You were miles away," she said.

"Well, I'm back here now," I said, "and happy to be so."

Over the steaming table of food we raised our glasses and chinked them together. The intimacy of the moment embarrassed us and we cleansed our palates with an insult or two over which we laughed, and then began eating. We talked as two girls talk, easy in each other's company. For the first time I forgot everything. I was happy. Isabel and I sitting together at the table, with a fire of apple logs crackling in the grate and the ceiling chandeliers lit for the first time she could remember.

I'd cooked the dinner, right down to the last bruised sprout; had cut the carrots into strips not roundels so as not to betray my origins; had removed the skins from chestnuts and dates, and the pips from thirty grapes. Phileda had put me in sole charge of Christmas. I had decorated the house expensively without recourse to a single toilet-roll angel or newspaper streamer. Because I had created it, Christmas was mine to give and Isabel accepted it like a visitor on her best behaviour. She took a child's delight in Christmas, which to me was a further sign of weakness. The candles threw pencils of light across her face. The room smelt of the damp moss and fir boughs I'd gathered in the moulting woods and placed above the fireplace. All the time there was a feeling that we were moving towards something; all the time I was overcoming my hesitancy, though I knew not why I hesitated.

The day before Christmas Eve, Phileda had received a letter from Geoffrey informing her that someone would be coming to pick up his car and the contents of his cellar, and could she make the keys available to both. Ever since, strange, invisible frictions had permeated the house. A feeling that we must walk on tiptoe or put black sheets over all the mirrors. Since the arrival of the letter, Phileda had made only brief appearances in the kitchen to refill her china teacup with lemon slices and hot water. A place had been laid for her at the dining table, with little expectation that she would fill it. Earlier in the day I'd crept along the landing, paused outside her door and heard the unmistakable *pock* of the foil seal breaking on a tablet packet. There had been no sign of her for the rest of the day. The floorboards creaked overhead as though a restless animal paced the confines of its cage. Isabel seemed oblivious to her mother's absence; the strangeness of the two of us dining alone on Christmas Day hadn't struck her.

Just as we were harmonising on the second verse of "Silent Night", the door opened and Phileda's face appeared, half in shadow, half in the red glow of the Christmas tree lights. Her face was pale and her brow corrugated like the iron sheets we used on the farm to patch up the holes in broken fences. There was something eerie about her too, as though her corporeal self had remained upstairs and this was her spirit come to deliver us an omen. She pushed open the door and stood swaying slightly on the threshold. She clutched something in her hand. It was Geoffrey's letter.

How we delude ourselves that the human mind can survive anything. It comes as a great source of strength and comfort to know that the brain is merely a muscle that needs to be worked to keep it bolstered from insanity. Making an ally of death helps to master the intellect. Then there is no fear. I saw in Phileda's face what I had always known: that she was full of fear. Her mind was also weak. The unmistakable breeze of strong drink moved with her into the room.

"Now, girls, seeing as it's Christmas, what d'you say we pay a visit to the cellar?" She spoke slowly and with forced lasciviousness. "Daddy would have wanted it." She hauled up a key on a chain from between her breasts, like a fish from a hole in the ice, and dangled it in front of my face.

Isabel looked aghast. I nudged her and whispered, "C'mon Is, this could be a riot."

The cellar was like all cellars. It smelt of death and damp, and a bare bulb lit the way down narrow steps. There were patches of burst plaster on the walls, around which powdery salts erupted. Down here Geoffrey kept his wine: the Mâcons, Médocs and Merlots arranged in brick bins around the walls; and then another door, iron-bound, with innumerable locks to confound the thief, beyond which lay his special selection. Phileda made straight for it. On the wall of the second, smaller room was a little case with a handwritten sign on the glass that said, "In Case of Emergency Break Here". Inside were a corkscrew and a crystal glass. Phileda told us it was Geoffrey's little joke. If the bomb dropped and he was forced to take refuge in the cellar, his worst fear was to be incarcerated without access to a corkscrew and a glass. If the bomb dropped, I imagined him smirking, thinking how clever he'd been to remember a corkscrew.

Taking off her shoe, Phileda smashed the glass with the spike of her heel and extracted the corkscrew. She inspected it closely, as though it was a bullet she'd removed with tweezers from a wound. Her fingers were determined: such pale, slender fingers. Beauty had rubbed off on them like a virus she'd caught from handling expensive, shop-bought objects. She began to take bottles off the shelves. "Let's see," she said to herself, and the vintage corks yielded to her tugs and did not put up any resistance in the way of cheap corks.

"This was a good year. Take a sip," she said, handing me a crystal goblet.

"Should you be doing that?" Isabel asked.

"Of course, darling. Good wine doesn't last for ever. What d'you say to this one?" she said, turning to me.

I put the glass to my lips and swallowed. "Immature, yet enthusiastic." Phileda giggled.

"Well, let's try another in that case, until we find one to our complete satisfaction."

"I hate it down here," said Isabel, pulling her cuffs over her hands. "I'm going back up."

"Bye, bye," said Phileda, giving her a sad look and a child's wave by opening and closing her fist like a star. It was obvious Isabel went not because of the cellar but because of her mother. The change in Phileda was like a dagger between them.

The enormous weight of the house above our heads suddenly seemed significant. Hanging on the walls of the cellar were the hallmarks of Geoffrey's occupation: a character-car calendar; a black-and-white photograph of him and the Prince of Wales shaking hands in front of an ivy-clad edifice, with Brillcreamed fringes swept from left to right; a joke postcard that said, "Golfers do it in bunkers"; a certificate for firearms. The sense of Geoffrey still belonging gave me a stitch in my side.

Phileda, meanwhile, was working her way through the racks of wine, opening bottles one after another. Some she poured and drank from; others she sniffed and discarded. A trail of corks and bottle-top wrappings littered the floor like metallic apple peelings. The ones she liked, she passed to me. I sipped, but not too much. I wanted to relish the tastes; to commit them to memory. And besides I was a connoisseur of what drink could do to a woman. It was beginning to take its toll on Phileda. The bare bulb did not flatter her: she had on too much blue eyeshadow, as if someone had once told her her eyes were her best feature and she must adorn them. She also wore a brighter shade of lipstick than usual; it made her look like one of the women out of Isabel's catalogue, like she was modelling a part in a pretend life.

The best of Geoffrey's wine was soon uncorked. Phileda looked pleased with herself. She sat down on a chair as if exhausted by the effort and waved for me to do likewise. I knew talk would come next because it always did and I thought how rarely conversation lived up to our expectations. The bare bulb cast a circle of Gestapo light over the table. She lent forward, knotting her fingers together. We were nearing a heart to heart. I imagined the bloodied organs sitting on the table vying for supremacy: whose was bigger; whose had suffered the most pain, while we pumped them from behind like toy frogs beset on winning a race.

"I've never told anyone this before . . ." But I knew she had, because I'd looked in her desk and had read the notes she'd scribbled to her psychiatrist. The notes on purple paper in which she'd asked, "What gave rise to me?" A litany of privilege ensued. She remembered her father's damp kisses; the family parties when none were needed; the unspoken veto on words such as "meal", "serviette", "afters". There were floral armchairs and cold game pie in the dark vault of her childhood. There was no one more menacing than a grandfather with side-burns, who'd made his mark as a judge with a reputation for leniency.

But then the following words came; words I had been waiting for, in some unfathomable way, since my arrival at Critchley Hall: "There was another child," she said. A pause of three breaths or perhaps three thousand breaths elapsed. This black pearl of information had been omitted from the notes: there was another child. Another child. Child. The shape of those four thin words in my hands: the texture of them and the infinite possibilities they afforded danced through my mind. The fiery light of revelation held up time.

"It's a painful subject," she said in a slow voice. "She died in her sleep, aged two years and four months. Isabel doesn't know she had a sister." Her face, lifted now to the burning bulb, bore the imprint of grief as though a tear-shaped pastry cutter had been pressed down upon it. "Geoffrey had his first affair shortly after we lost her. We called her Amelia." She reached for her glass and drank deeply, a parody of a smile in red wine staining the corners of her mouth. "There's something about you that reminds me of her."

I tried to remember my own mother's face, but her features had receded to the point of no recall. For

96

evermore my own mother would lie just beyond this moment: on the other side of grasping fingertips, dull, dimmed and finally replaced. The shape of those four thin words. In my hands I would transform them.

# CHAPTER
# SIX

Dear Di(arrhoea)

I'm sorry I left without saying goodbye properly. Always been bad at *adieus* (French). That last bit with Mum was kind of sad, don't you think? And I couldn't bear another row. I think the poor old badger needs help but I'm not the one to give it. If she were a dog I'd take her to the vet right away and have her put out of her misery. Pouring port into the petrol tank of Dad's car was just *de trop* (French). Not even funny. Just kind of desperate. Sixth-form college is Dullsville in comparison, but I couldn't stand another minute of her antics. And anyway, I've got to resit my exams if "I'M TO GET ANYWHERE IN THE WORLD" and avoid ending up in a secretarial college. I'm sharing a berth with a rather creepy girl called Emma. You'd loathe her. She, like me, has a silver spoon in her mouth, only the difference is hers is EPNS and mine is hallmarked — an obvious breeding ground for the baser emotions but I'll have her beat before the week's out.

The corridors here smell rather disgustingly of rubberbands and testosterone, and most of the men have only just learned to walk upright, but apart from that the place is tolerable. Except, without you here, I've got no one to tell my dreams to, which is a pity because they're rather challenging at the moment. The sheets are always in a tangle when I wake up. Perhaps I'm breathing in too much of this Emma girl's air. She lives on honey sandwiches and insists on playing classical music on her cassette player. See what I mean about her?

Bless you, *ma petite soeur*, for taking on the role of surrogate. I'm fond of the mother goose but I just can't live with her. I hope she gives you a good time in Venice, you deserve it, after everything. It's just up your cul-de-sac. Though the thought of sharing a hotel room with her gives me the shivers. You are brave. I miss you, of course, but don't let it go to your head. Write me by return.

Yours everest

Is

My first holiday abroad. Phileda smiled when she heard this. It was what persuaded her to take me. "You'll love Venice," she said. "It's like nowhere else on earth." She confessed she had been spoilt by too much travel at an early age; had become indifferent to it: one church façade was much the same as another; a cobbled street was a cobbled street; bad manners the same wherever you went. "I often feel lost in foreign cities," she said on our way to the airport, "but Venice is different, familiar somehow." She'd honeymooned there in 1965. Another reason for the return.

I was determined to loathe Venice because everyone had said I would love it. I did my best on first glimpse, floating up the Grand Canal, jostled by tourists who covered their faces with cameras as though they were gas masks and reality a fume that might overwhelm them. I persuaded myself that the buildings edging the water had been built to be licked not lived in; that the windows pocking the coloured façades were holes where teeth had rotted due to a diet of spun sugar. But despite my best efforts of resistance the city's true beauty soon began to take hold. The vaporetto drew us up the aisle of water as though to an altar. The sun on the palazzo walls brought the water alive. Then, and only then, was the water stroked with the colours of ripening fruit. Elsewhere, in the shadows, the water moved through the city like a spinach slick.

We stayed in a hotel that had entertained royalty and filmstars in its time. The shabby façade was an indication of refinement, not neglect. The foyer walls were covered with photographs of people too famous to need names. Giant pots of lilies, dove flesh of the flower world, perfumed the conditioned air. While Phileda wandered off to find the "powder room", the receptionist asked me whether my mother would require newspapers in the morning. I said she would and that I liked my boiled eggs hard.

Our twin-bedded room was filled with bamboo furniture and the walls were decorated with laurel sprigs in diamond-shaped motifs. The window blinds and the bedcovers replicated this pattern. I told Phileda how much I loathed decor that matched and she laughed and said what an unusual girl I was. I felt pleased when she said that. So pleased, it was necessary to hide my face behind an in-flight magazine that had joined us from the plane. There was a sitting room attached to the bedroom with views across to San Giorgio Maggiore, and a tray for making cocktails. There was also embossed writing paper and two small bottles of spring water by the side of our beds. Already I could feel the room's brightness fusing into me, as though the laughter of the last guests lingered in the folds of the curtains.

That first night we dined in the restaurant of the hotel. Waiters with helmet-shaped haircuts waltzed across the polished floors, with trays poised on the tips of four fingers. Phileda's indifference had them fawning. Conversely, my solicitude irritated them. For the first time since the Geoffrey affair, Phileda's eyes shone. Two females travelling alone: the mother needing solace, the daughter needing entertainment; there was legitimate reason for the waiters to heap upon us the surreptitious compliments of the house. She said: "We'll have fun here you and I." Out of the window, the boat traffic bobbed and the dimming light bled onto the faraway buildings like yesterday's glow, sad and not in its first flush of youth.

Later, back in our room, Phileda changed into a sleeveless nightgown and prepared for bed. Her upper arms were labelled with the indents of childhood injections. Having kissed me goodnight on the cheek, she then did something I was unprepared for — something which surprised me. She dropped to her knees upon the hard floor and with her elbows on the bed, she began to pray. I hadn't seen a person pray out of chapel before. It didn't make me laugh. To laugh at something was to show you hadn't been affected by it. But I had been affected by it. Phileda believed in God. Seeing her on her knees was like witnessing a creation: an act outside itself in which she put herself willingly at the mercy of a greater good. I hung back in the shadows of the curtain and strained to hear her whispered words. I heard Amelia's name and Isabel's too. It was the closest I'd come to true goodness. I suppose because opposites attract, my hand moved of its own accord towards the wave of dark hair so recently loosened from its clip. If I reached out and touched, surely smoke would rise from my fingertips and my flesh would burn. Someone in the street below shouted goodbye without using a word for it. A motor revved into life. My hand hovered like a drowsy insect in mid-air and then retreated.

That night I slept restlessly. The sound of the wavelets, lapping the bellies of the moored gondolas, cracked like applause down the deserted canalways. The dark sea and the danger beyond; never had water seemed less enticing to swimmers.

The next day Phileda bought me a camera in a shop behind the Rialto Bridge. I tried to beat the shop assistant down on price but Phileda waved me to one side, taking a slab of smooth, new banknotes from her bag and paying the man the money he desired. I remembered the occasions of shopping with my mother — the humiliation of keeping the new shoes on — the old ones with flapping soles taken away by the shop assistant between thumb and forefinger, as though they were rags that had been used to wipe the creamy sores of lepers. New meant cheap and never the thing you wanted. Perhaps my face gave too much away.

Outside, Phileda touched my hair. The giving had pleased her; the taking had pleased me even more. Her life, so fruitlessly rich, had doubled back on itself to the point where buying had lost its lustre and giving was the new drug. The camera hung on a plaid strap round my neck. I wore it proudly as though I had deserved it.

I took pictures all over the city. We climbed the campaniles; took boat rides to the little islands and, turning, saw the outline of the city etch the sky. We visited churches. We saw the walnut cherubs with dust in their eyes and the sad madonnas. I didn't count myself a tourist because I didn't take pictures of the sights. I took pictures of Phileda. Phileda happy, tired, hungry; Phileda consulting her guide-book, her watch, the interior of her handbag. If I caught a bridge or a building in the frame it was accidental. I saw the city out of the corner of my eye. But Phileda I had in perfect focus. We went everywhere together. I felt as confident and as assured as the city looked, striding down the narrow alleyways in Isabel's borrowed clothes. We never spoke of her. Strange how even then, we knew that the very mention of her name could spoil things for us; could tear our new-found closeness apart.

There was nobody I missed. Everything I had ever desired was compacted in the palm of my hand. Phileda made me believe that mine was the only company she desired. For the first time in my life trust took root like a weed in a gutter, blocking the pipe through which my childhood pain had previously flowed. It was like learning to swim: the moment when you let go of the side and realise you are afloat.

There was only one incident that almost scraped the paint off our holiday together. One evening we were dining in a little restaurant on the Campo dei Frari that overlooked the brick façade of a Franciscan church. Its simplicity fanned the eye after a day filled with too much baroque. Phileda was relaxed and happy, and ordered a second bottle of Amarone. We dined on *antipasti*: a large plate between us, crammed full of glistening peppers and anchovies, roasted fennel and thin slices of *prosciutto*. Hard bread turned to soft when dipped in the silky juice of the olive oil. Phileda glowed; she was like a flag unfurled, released from the constraints of Critchley. We talked about the sinking city and the bells: how mournful they could sound and yet how beautiful. A wayward third button of her shirt had come undone and the line of a sunburned breast was just visible beneath the lift of white linen. She hadn't brushed her hair since lunchtime and it gave her a reckless look. I poured more wine. She was talking animatedly, throwing her arms around and laughing loudly. The second bottle arrived. The waiter, with a flourish, told us it came with the compliments of the gentleman sitting in the corner, over there. A young Italian lifted his hand at us but did not smile.

"Oh, you lucky girl," said Phileda. "Look, he's gorgeous."

"Phileda!" I bleated. "What can you mean?"

"Don't looked so shocked," she said, laughing, "I was young once, too, you know. I feel a holiday romance coming on." And she looked into the distance, as though remembering her first sandy-lipped kiss beneath an awning of desert stars. "Go and speak to him," she said.

"No way."

"Then I will," and she got to her feet.

"Phileda, please . . ." I squeaked, my voice two octaves higher than I meant it to be, but she was already walking towards him across the room, her bracelets leaving a scent of warm brass around my face.

The sounds of the restaurant were suddenly magnified: the clatter of a metal tray on the kitchen floor, the buzz of conversation, the snigger of the till as it printed out receipts. I could hardly breathe. I felt like the narrator of a story I'd lost the strength to tell. I had no appetite for words but I was hungry for pictures: the simple, visual pleasure of watching Phileda move across the room towards the stranger in the corner. But it was not a picture I had drawn. The strokes were coarse and lacked the subtlety of finer detail. I dreaded what might happen.

She reached his table and bent down towards him. I saw him sneak a look between the folds of her open shirt. Her fingers chastely brought the flaps of fabric together and closed around the escaped button. She spoke to him and there was shy laughter between them.

His skin was the colour of Georgian mahogany kept out of the sun; his eyes blue and small like those of deep-water fish. I saw him shake his head and smile. He pointed vaguely towards her neck and his lips said: "*Bellisima.*" She took a step away from him. She blushed, she pushed her fingers through her hair and I, sitting alone at the crumb-encrusted table, thought how few surprises there were in life.

Phileda came back to the table flushed with the exertion of finding herself desirable. Without looking at me she said, "He's not for you," and consoled herself with a gulp of wine. I felt myself reverting; felt foolish and discarded but smiled through it. I reached out and held my finger in the candle flame. "Ouch, don't do that," said Phileda. But I felt nothing, nothing but a faint glow that was, in its own way, pleasurable.

He was waiting outside the restaurant when we left. She said, "You go on back to the hotel. I'll be with you in a moment."

Wild horses were running loose in my head. There was confusion and dust. This was Phileda with a new purpose. Phileda who'd suddenly outgrown the clothes I'd given her to wear. I needed time to think. But I didn't have time; I had to act quickly. The Italian was leaning against the side of a well outside the restaurant. Phileda fell into conversation with him. I walked on, past the little shop that sold notebooks and where I'd planned to come back to tomorrow. I turned a corner and could see the row of blue umbrellas outside our hotel. A putrid smell of rotting fish rose up from the adjoining canal and mingled with the smell of pizza.

The alleyway I found myself in was full of discarded cabbage leaves and crumbling render. I thought for a moment about what I would do, then retraced my steps. Phileda was still where I had left her talking to the Italian and picking a stone out of her flip-flop. She grabbed at his arm to steady herself. I was running out of time but an idea was forming.

I ran back to the reception of the hotel and returned with the porter. I pointed Phileda out. "Please tell the *signora* to come back to the hotel immediately," I said. "Tell her her friend is ill." I pressed a note into his hand and ran back to our room. I locked myself in the bathroom and turned on the taps.

When she returned there were sympathy and lies. The anchovies were blamed. She said a trip was all it was; he wanted to take her to the Academia to see the Carpaccios: a Virgin, in particular, who reminded him of her. I ran to the bathroom, pretending to be sick again. I came out dryly dabbing at my mouth. I told her it was dangerous, going off with a man she didn't know; that I had reservations. I told her no matter how nice they seemed, men were unpredictable: there were swells and gusts in all of them not visible to the naked eye. And I should know, given my recent experience. She flinched when I said this, her face sad suddenly, like something long settled in a bottle.

She said, "My God, how could I be so thoughtless." She sat down heavily on the edge of the bed, and felt my brow and then my cheek. "You're so young to know such things." I had a sense of arrival, of doors opening and jugs being filled. "What was I thinking?" she said, her words like a patent giving me the right. "You rescued me." I closed my eyes and leaned back against the pillows. "I didn't mean to worry you." The softness of the night air. "I won't leave you again, I promise." I felt the imprint of her lips on the back of my hand.

It was the following morning. I remember the moment exactly. I was in St Mark's Square, close to the arched colonnade of the Doge's Palace. I looked up at the clock on the Torre dell'Orologio. It was eight thirty. I was photographing a dead pigeon because there was still life in it. What is death if not still life in all its painterly forms? The sky was already blue — no clouds, only gusts of live pigeons that flew up into the air like blown rubbish. But the dead pigeon lay there, next to a white napkin that someone had discarded from a takeaway meal. The napkin was its shroud. Its wing touched it almost tenderly. Beads of bright blood pillowed its head and shoulder. More so in death was this life beautiful.

The hordes of other pigeons gathered round the early seed stalls in the square. One or two clambered onto the heads and shoulders of likely feeders. The rest strutted across the flagstones like nodding dogs, a comic sight and not a patch on my pigeon, who through death had finally become something — had attained a form of immortality. I clicked and framed. Clicked and framed, while the bells of St Mark's tolled a requiem for the dead bird. Then I caught sight of Phileda rushing out of a side alley towards me. I knew it had to be something bad. She wasn't properly dressed and never went anywhere without her handbag. She wore the dazed look of someone who has just been saved from a burning building. I was on my knees before the pigeon, having just had my ear to its breast while listening for a heartbeat. Phileda was burbling and not making much sense. "I don't know how to tell you," she began. "A phone call. Something's happened."

Picturing Isabel I said, "What?" wishing she would get to the point.

She drew her lips into her mouth, sealing them with a finger. "There's only one way to tell you. Your mother is ill, seriously ill. They don't know whether she'll last the day out."

I turned back to the pigeon and continued photographing. The blood was beginning to halo like a sunrise behind its head and I did not want to miss it. Phileda reached over and took the camera from me. Somewhere in a shoebox I have a photograph of the inside of her hand. She laid the camera aside and then crouched down and put her arms around me; the pigeon between us. The toe of her shoe caught the edge of the napkin. I wanted her to move it but I couldn't find the words to ask. A small dog with a bow in its hair raised its hind leg on a column of the Doge's Palace. I rested my head gently on Phileda's shoulder.

"Amelia, Amelia," she said. "Oh my dear, Amelia."

We cut our holiday short. My mother made a complete recovery. But before she did, I visited her in hospital. Phileda dropped me off. I stood for ages after she'd gone in the beam of the automatic doors with a pot plant in my hands, wishing I was somewhere else. I was afraid that if I went into the hospital and sat by her bed she would reinfect me with every kind of poverty. The automatic doors opened and closed, opened and closed, wafting out the smell of recently cleaned-up vomit and disinfectant. There were people in a line outside smoking. People with tubes coming out of them in wheelchairs, eating crisps and passing round wrappered sweets. Through the finger-smudged glass I could see a woman with no legs being helped from one chair to another by two men, who linked her under her arms.

I went in. I wore my good health like a magic mantle: it would protect me from infection; it made me feel superior. A path opened up through the sick people for me to walk down. I must have imagined it. They shaded their eyes, they raised their sticks in admiration, dazzled by the pure white lines of my well-being. I felt beautiful and strong in a world full of people made ugly and weak by sickness.

My mother made barely a rumple in the bedclothes. She lay with her face turned to the window. At the sound of my step she turned her head. "I knew you'd come," she said. "I'm like a dog. I have a sixth sense." Her face was older. That gave me a twinge. The bags under her eyes had grown larger, like cushions her tired eyes rested upon. Her hands were cleaner than I'd ever seen them. We sat and faced each other over the sepulchral smoothness of the bedclothes. She waved a hand and said, "In here, they're all fighting the truth of their diagnosis." She gave a cynical laugh and heaved herself up against a mound of flat pillows. "Believe," she said, tapping my hand. "Just believe."

Believe what? I thought. She'd always gone in for big gesture presentiments that were borne out of nothing other than her need to attract attention by making herself sound fey. I put the plant down next to a jug of cloudy water. I looked hard into her face to see if I could see anything of myself there. There was not a single possession of hers to be seen. Even her nightie was National Health, tied on by two strings at the back of her neck. I looked through the window. Outside was a clean world separate from my mother. A woman was reversing a car out of the carpark. A small group had gathered round. The men were laughing; the women sympathising. There were swings and children playing and dogs barking. The sound of them depressed me. The mark beneath the swing, where their feet had scuffed, patched the field like a puncture repair. I followed the outline of it, round and round.

"What did you have to do for that necklace?" she asked, her left eye tilted towards me like a chicken's. I smiled, and my smile heralded the tink of sword tips before the contest begins. But this contest was finished long before it had even begun. We two were cracked from the same egg; the same eternal spring had fed us. Our histories had made us. In my heart I felt nothing. I had nothing to fear. The scent of the pot plant reached me. Phileda had brought it up from the glasshouse. It was a geranium. The trick was not to water them too frequently, she'd said. They liked dry soil.

"It was a present."

"Presents come with a price tag where I come from," she said.

She asked about Critchley. Did I see much of Mrs de Burgh? What was it like sleeping in a high bed? Had I found a pea beneath the mattress yet? If I kept up the accent, soon I'd be able to read the news. The scythe-sweep of her words fell against me but did not knock me down.

"Can't you be pleased for me?" I said. She turned away. She looked like a prisoner trying to resist confession, no emotion on her face; implacable. Then another thought entered her head and her eyes brightened. I braced myself.

"And Mr de Burgh?" she asked gently, coaxing. "I'd heard she'd kicked him out. Was it anything to do with you?"

I bit my lip, tasted blood, blushed. A slow, victorious smile spread across her face. I felt doomed and sad; sad in a way only mothers can make you; because I couldn't decide what was worse — the uncanny knack she had of knowing or the pleasure she took in drawing blood.

Above the bed my mother's surname was written on a wipe-clean board; underneath, the ghosts of other names leached through in blue felt pen. "I'm not coming back," I said. Her hands searched for an invisible magazine between the bedclothes, closing down, shutting off. She didn't believe me. I didn't believe myself.

There was nothing to be gained by staying. The cloudy perfume of Phileda's geranium threw out an anchor and landed in me. My mother's hands, the pear-shaped lobes of her ears, the way her hair sprouted on her forehead in a V slightly off centre to her nose, the mole I knew was there at the base of her neck — I shrugged off their significance like a jumper I'd outgrown. Someone in the next ward began to moan. Nothing could hurt that much my mother said. I got up to leave, feeling her eyes assessing how much I'd grown. "By the way," she said, as I walked away from the bed, "your cat's dead."

I ran the rest of the way out of the hospital and the wet-look floors of the corridors seemed like long tunnels down which I fell. I had loved my cat very much and yet I had abandoned her to a lonely old age without me. People shouted at me to slow down. Phileda was parked outside the emergency unit in a bay marked for doctors. She was sorting through her handbag on the passenger seat.

"You're upset," she said, with concern in her voice. I was surprised how glad I was to see her; to hear again the scrupulous pronunciation of vowel and consonant that had until recently irritated me. The children playing on the swings looked over to see who climbed into the sleek black car that could only be a drug pusher's, could only be a rock star's off his patch. "Your mother's in the best place possible," she said, misunderstanding completely.

We drove back with the roof down. Phileda put a tape on. It was a warm day but with crisp shadows and a lushness in the fields only spring could produce. I closed my eyes, charting my journey from the smell of the hedgerows. What I didn't say on the way back, Schubert's *Winterreise* said for me, and the engine roared below the music: a raft of deeper sound upon which the sweeter notes floated. I felt Phileda's eyes on my face each time she changed gear — the same lovely feeling as feigning an illness to escape school and the ruse working, and the thought of a whole empty day stretching ahead. I hoped the journey would go on for ever and with it the idea of being borne along in safety. The rumble of the cattle grid, the air cooler in the shadows beneath the beech trees, the scent of azaleas. And then Phileda's voice saying, "Wake up, darling, we're home."

# CHAPTER
# SEVEN

The months before Isabel came back to Critchley were the happiest of my life. But there is no happiness that does not leave a shadow. It was the hottest spring I could remember. Old Popey, the gardener, did nothing but complain about the brown lawns. There were damp dribbles across the paths where the hosepipe had crossed. The scent of wild garlic carried up from the woods. I amused myself by making speciality bread and by growing as many different kinds of lettuce as I could find seeds for. There was novelty in growing things for waste. I overfed the fish. I lounged with Josy on the sunbleached boards of the drawing room, my head near her stomach, pacing two, wheezy, fur-balled breaths for one of each of mine.

I'd unplugged the telephone in Phileda's bedroom. When it rang downstairs I said she was out or asleep. Voices you could stir with a spoon said tell her to phone back; I didn't, and soon they stopped ringing. One time I got to the phone on its ninth ring. I held the receiver to my ear. Silence. "Is that you, Is?" I said. I tried to listen for a clue beneath the quiet: radio mumble or music. But really I didn't need a clue to tell me who it was. The silence was angry; it was beyond what words

**115**

could do to calm it. I knew it was Geoffrey. The line went dead.

On my way back up to the attic, Phileda called me into her bedroom. It was the first time I'd been into her room with her in it. I knew it well without her, had combed it like a beach while she was out: had fingered every object, stroked the surface of every belonging — like the little Chinese bowl she kept her rings in, and the rings themselves. Someone had once told me that to know everything about an object was to possess it. The same applied with people. Objects made you belong in the world. Belongings were the pegs that kept you pinned to the earth. Being and longing: to exist and to yearn; sensing yourself alive. I'd also looked in her drawers and in the bottom of cupboards where the forgotten things lived among a tangle of belts and shoes and broken coat hangers. Nothing escaped me. Once, forgetting, I almost told her where Isabel's lost silver bracelet was. It was in the bottom drawer of a little lacquered cabinet, beneath a stash of Geoffrey's old love letters in which he'd staked his claim on her heart, using words like "utmost" and "eventually".

I hadn't seen her since lunchtime. She usually had a nap after lunch and some days I wouldn't see her again until the following morning, when she would appear in the kitchen, dry-mouthed and shadowed, saying she felt better for a good night's sleep. That evening all the windows were open because of the heat. The house smelled of darkness: of dew and foxes and warm bark.

I turned the handle and went in. She was lying on the bed fully clothed, as still as a stone saint, with a pale

**116**

gauze scarf wrapped round her head. I could see the dark pools of her eyes and the dip where her mouth was; the straps of her shoes were undone. I wished I'd had my camera. A moth had left streaks of itself on the lampshade. She was breathing quickly. Her blouse had risen up and I could see her stomach; it looked like a field with its dips and rises. Once, I'd have thought it an excellent surface for my plastic toy horses to play on. I'd have filled up her belly button with water from my pipette for the horses to drink from. But childish things had put me aside. Now I just looked and marvelled at its strange translucence that shimmered like snow or any surface you could sink your hands into.

The head in the scarf spoke: "I can't move," it said. "I detest things that crawl. They simply terrify me." Cherry blossom had blown into the room from the open window. It made the room look lonely. I couldn't see whatever creature she was referring to. Nothing moved or rippled. The room was monotonously still and tidy: hung up, folded, shelved; her sweaters in the cupboard stacked in such a way that they begged for a jumbling hand.

"There's nothing," I said.

"It's over there on the windowsill. I can hear it. It's eating a leaf or something." I went over to the windowsill. There was a large straw hat with a butterfly brooch pinned to its brim. She wore it in the garden.

"Phileda, there's nothing," I said again. But as I watched the butterfly brooch shivered and came alive, opening its wings stiffly from the furry hinge of its body. It high-stepped along the edge of the brim, its legs like strokes on a music score. The intense glow from the overhead light and the heat in the room had dizzied it almost to death. I picked it up easily. It spun like a grounded Spitfire in the palm of my hand. Then I comprehended that this small thing with wings was the root of Phileda's fear.

"Kill it, kill it," came the muffled cry from inside the scarf, "take my shoe." I covered the butterfly with my hands and took it to the window. Its wings brushed the inside cup of my fingers. I blew it off, launching it into the night like a toy boat with sails. "I've killed it," I said. "Look, it's gone."

She pulled the scarf gingerly from her eyes and I danced my empty hands in the air like a magician after making a dove disappear. She groaned with relief. All the air in her body seemed to go from her. Her voice trembled when she whispered her thanks. She took a crumpled tissue from beneath her pillow and held it to her temple. She asked for some whisky. I got her some from downstairs and finger-stepped the banister on the way back up, feeling young, strong and irresponsible. I was back where I wanted to be: filling space, not just falling through air like most people but making things matter, making every second count. Phileda told me she had lain like that for two hours. She'd read of commandos in the Vietnam War who'd become the jungle by lying still and had, in that way, avoided detection. Her aim had been to stop the butterfly noticing her. She was afraid it might be attracted to the floral sprigs on her skirt.

118

Later, when her trembling had ceased, she asked me if I would move out of Isabel's room into the green room, next to hers — in case. "In case what?" I asked.

"I can't say," she replied. "I just have a feeling, you know, of perhaps sometimes needing someone."

A pink rose in a vase dropped its petals on the bedside table. She frowned and then went back to scrunching up the bedclothes and letting them fall, making tiny eruptions in the satin eiderdown. She had a needing, wanting look on her face. A flood of contentment bled outwards from the centre of my stomach.

It wasn't long after the incident with the butterfly that the "offering" appeared. It was as if it had been a prelude to something worse. It was morning. The house was quiet, only the ticking of clocks and the shudder of the fridge, as it cooled, then warmed, in the kitchen. I unlocked the porch door and went out to take my first breath of morning air. Phileda was still sleeping upstairs. She rarely stirred before ten. I was thinking that today I'd sweep the leaves off the tennis court, put a bat in Phileda's hand and see what happened. I anticipated the scene with a smile. The air was clear, crisp. I preferred the air cold before the sun warmed it, before it tasted used. I thought of Isabel's wardrobe and what I would wear today. She had all the gear for tennis: the little skirts with their pleats as stiff as cardboard, the green-peaked visors and the stretchy tops. I would choose. I'd have fun and the sun would stroke me.

I must have stood on the step for at least a minute before I realised what was at my feet. The first gift was from Josy. It was a mole. Its body was unblemished except for a small speck of blood which covered the tip of its nose. Its coat was velvet-soft and black like night without a moon, and it seemed a miracle that a creature so clean, so manicured, could live beneath the soil. Its paws were turned outwards in a pose of supplication. Brave little man, I knew Phileda would say; animals were always personified, except when she was slipping them into her mouth from the end of a fork. I contemplated taking the mole to her, imagined the shock, the screams that would ensue.

It was then that I noticed the bunch of roses leaning up against the doorframe. For a moment I just stared at them, wondering how this message from the outside world had crept into our lives and what it meant. I looked towards the sweep of trees that surrounded the back of the house, expecting a further sign, an answer. It says a lot about my happy state of mind at the time that I thought they were for me. For a fleeting second I felt like a brave young god come to gather up his gifts. I saw inside the cellophane cone a small square of card. I fished it out excitedly. It said: "Phileda, I'm sorry. Please forgive me. G". I didn't immediately understand. And when I did, my own stupidity appalled me. The flowers were not meant for me.

I reached down and picked up the mole and held it against my face for comfort. The dense, trimmed softness of the coat and the movement of little bones beneath my fingers reassured me. In the dust where the gravel had worn away I could see a footprint. Geoffrey had been here. I imagined him skulking round the house while we were snug inside; could almost hear the rasp of his waxed jacket as he moved, and his powdery, dry breaths like an animal that uses its nose to forage. I looked again towards the trees. Nothing. Only the vaguest whisper of a breeze moving through the leaves below a crab-pink sky.

I needed a moment to think. First, I would dispose of Geoffrey's gift. I walked round to the horses' field with the roses in my hand. I carried them, not in the usual manner, like a baby cradled in the hook of the arm, but more like a truncheon ready for assault. Darius and Hester were waiting by the gate. I climbed up in front of them and sat on the top bar. "Darius," I said, "do you take Hester to be your lawful wedded wife?" I pressed Darius's head up and down. His forelock flapped loosely between his ears. "Hester, do you take Darius to be your lawful wedded husband?" She too nodded assent at the push of my hand. "Then I pronounce you man and wife."

I undid the cellophane from the roses. A scent of cardboard: hard, flat. The blooms twisted easily off their stems; they came away like knuckles out of sockets, leaving a yellow crown, a circle of raised filaments on the tip of each stalk. Each bloom was a tight knot of colour in my hand. I threw the petals into the air; they took flight like a charm of small, bloodied finches and landed on the horses' heads, on their backs, became entangled in their manes, confetti showering their union, a smattering of red against the black and the grey.

There were some petals left. I filled my pockets with them. I took the long way back to the house through a little copse of wellingtonias and past the glasshouses which no one used any more. There was a smell of moss and decay; I'd smelt it before in towns, the places where people couldn't get to, behind cinemas or supermarkets: the smell of leaves and blown rubbish. Each time I thought of Geoffrey I took a handful of petals from my pocket and threw them up into the air. To me Geoffrey was dead, finished, and the petals were his ashes which I scattered now in the forgotten places of the garden.

By the time I got back to the house, I knew what to do. I went into the study where Phileda kept the house paperwork. On the desk there was a brass paperclip in the shape of a crocodile. In its mouth was Geoffrey's new address. I tore his card in two and placed it in an envelope. In Phileda's hand, I wrote his address on the envelope. Tomorrow I would post it. He was not the kind of man to beg for forgiveness a second time.

. . . who knows, maybe I'll have more to report when I write next. He's nice. Funny. He wears shoes with laces and he has a tiny scar on the left side of his nose that he got when he fell off a space hopper onto a tree root. He gave me a small, stuffed elephant the other day. Sweet? Yes, I thought so too. It's nice knowing someone away from the campus and there's the bonus of his job and car. His tiny blond curls have an appetising way of springing back into place when they're pulled. Shall I go on? OK, if you insist. He's an auctioneer, works for a local firm, but really he's a poet. He's always scribbling. He writes poems about me. Not embarrassing poems, no, they're beautiful and deep . . . beyond me in many ways. AND HE DOESN'T TOUCH ME. He says our love must spring from the evolution of the spirit not the senses. How rare, how pretty. But I can see he wants to. He's a master of self-control. Sometimes I wish he wasn't so good. Sometimes I can feel myself burning up just sitting next to him and I don't know what to do with the feeling. It seems a waste somehow. But I sense he's trying hard to restore my faith in *man*kind. I don't know how he knows it needs restoring.

I saw Dad the other night. He told me things about the "event" with you that I didn't believe. His lying made it much, much worse. He said it hadn't been entirely his fault. I told him I didn't want to see him again until he could come to terms with what he had done — until he took full responsibility for his actions. He looked so sad. But I didn't fall for it. It doesn't matter now if I never see him again. I shouted that after him, as he walked away through the swing doors of the hotel.

Thanks for setting my mind at ease about Mum. There's a lot of it going around. Everyone's ill here.

I miss you — let it go to your head.

Isabel x

I was delighted with my new quarters: the room next to Phileda's. It was a priority guestroom, reserved, in Geoffrey's time, for men who wore signet rings on their little fingers, who brought wives with them only to make up a fourth in bridge. It had a four-poster bed hung in green and gold brocade, and if I plumped up the pillows high enough I could line up the top of the dressing-table mirror with the sundial and the obelisk beyond. It had that bleached feel to it: south facing and faintly reminiscent of the cocktail hour; the carpet dark round the edges, pale in the centre; watercolours of deserted lochs; sun-warped shutters; empty perfume bottles on the dressing table still with their old-rose bouquet. Each night, not expecting to sleep, I slept. Each morning, I woke, bandaged in the mint-cool of linen sheets; the scent of old-world luxury rinding the inside of my nostrils.

When I could persuade Phileda out of her room, there were funny times when we'd be mad together and have mad conversations sitting in odd places around the house, or in the gardens that were full of places designed to be mad in — like the shell grotto or the coracle house, which was half a boat sticking out of the earth with a seat in it. Conversations that went like this:

"D'you know how easy it is to breathe underwater?"

"Don't be ridiculous, no one can breathe underwater, only fish and perhaps mermaids."

"How sweet, Amelia, you believe in mermaids."

"Don't you?" thinking it was just the kind of thing she'd believe in.

"I believe in all kinds of things but not mermaids. Once I believed in love — see how impressionable I was? Easier to believe in mermaids. Imagine all those scales. What would you do if you had an itch? You'd itch it, I suppose. Why did the mermaid blush?"

"I don't know. Why did the mermaid blush?"

"Because the sea weed." And she laughed until it ended in a coughing fit.

They were the best times, when I could be natural with her and not have to put on an act or worry about what she was thinking of me. She talked endlessly about Geoffrey. Every day there was a new photo to discuss or a gift would be produced that he had given her to atone: a handbag from Dubai or a Tiffany heart.

Time in slow motion, the way astronauts walked on the moon. A weekday afternoon was like a Saturday over and over. Boredom, blissful and becoming; the sweat of hot, airless nights disguised in freesia the following morning. Lunch at three; tea at five: marquetry trays balanced on the clipped shelf of a yew hedge, a tartan blanket and a breeze, thank God. Books left out overnight: a slug trail over Lehman, Taylor and *The Sorrows of Young Werther*.

Phileda, adrift in her matelessness, lying back on the grass. She wore dresses now, loose and expanding, flowered cheesecloth forgotten since the Isle of Wight;

the spit of a Van Eyck bride with her arched eyebrows and high, small breasts outlined beneath the fabric. She told me about the boyfriends she'd had before Geoffrey: a jump jockey and a croupier. Lack of love made her nostalgic for love. The latter with his soft, considerate hands; the former's quickness.

Whatever I told her, I made up, squinting against the sun while I said it. I told her nothing. I was too young for a past. Guilt at my deceit lay like a hand on my shoulder. But lies were irresistible. The more I could hide, the stronger I became. She seemed to have forgotten the thing between Geoffrey and I. Not forgotten, buried. It was simpler that way. Hence, my name change. Hence, Amelia.

She'd do whatever I asked. Anything, especially if it made me laugh. How stupid could I make her look? Tapping my fingers on my cheek, I asked her to sing "I'm a Little Teapot". "Go on," I said, "do it for me." And she did. She got up off the lawn and kicked off her sandals, and in her out-of-tune voice she sang, "I'm a little teapot short and stout", accompanied by the actions, putting one hand on her hip, the other arcing up and down like a teapot, pouring. She did it without any sign of embarrassment. "Tip me up and pour me out." And I knew she'd have done the same in front of an audience of two hundred, and afterwards made a little curtsey and given a hesitant little smile just as she did for me now. She'd slid down the tunnel of her mother's womb with the same surety, just as Isabel had slid out of hers. I, however, had baulked at playing

Mary in the school nativity play, had given myself a rash just thinking about it.

Phileda would do anything in her current state of mind. That was how families like hers and Geoffrey's became privileged. By doubling and daring, by shaking the dice, by running out into a sea of Zulus yelling for God and for Empire, with only one shot left in the barrel. For that you got a rose named after you. Courage and arrogance were the antecedents of stupidity in my book.

There were boxes of papers in the attic: tea chests, trunks and cardboard boxes full of family papers. All the stuff someone had thought to keep over the years, rolled up, stacked and rubber-banded with posterity in mind. Handwriting crossed over handwriting; black-edged cards, "my humblest apologies" beneath a broken seal of a stag's head, caboshed. A whole room was devoted to these papers. It was the hottest place in the house. Josy often came up with me for this reason. A dormer window emerged from the roof like the drawer of an open filing cabinet. We were higher than the swallows' nests under the eaves, higher than the tops of trees.

On a day when there was nothing else to do and the air was liquid with the sound of birds, I began to work my way through the boxes. At first the process was one of identification: Mary de Burgh née Cavendish on the evening of her betrothal to Cecil. She wrote from the steamer, *Enterprise*, on her way to the Americas: ". . . my heart is fit to burst at the thought of leaving dear Papa and Blink but my new life must begin

**127**

somewhere". Two first-class tickets and a white glove, unworn. "The people are dark-skinned and sing strange hymns . . ."

There were other letters too, mostly from battlefields, reminding me that history was true after all. Letters from Mons, Ladysmith, Sebastopol, Waterloo. The older the letter the thicker the paper until, falling through the centuries, we landed on parchment, stiff and unyielding; the demesne was bought. There were codicils and covenants and locks of fair hair; there were tarnished wedding rings and licks of rainbow colour from the ribbons of medals. And there were photographs of family members, remote and wide-eyed, as if they couldn't shake sleep from their heads, but all with the same look of haughtiness around the mouth that comes from occupying the same piece of land for centuries. Like trees with firm roots they grew up and bore fruit. I reminded myself that they were all dead but that I was not and a strong enough wind could uproot them. My strength lay in what I could forget, not in what I could remember.

Josy stretched out among the scatter of papers on the floor. There was one last box. I lifted the lid. A photograph of Isabel stared up at me. Isabel as a child, looking right into the camera, not smiling. Isabel parodying a grown-up in her mother's high heels, with lipsticked mouth. Isabel with plaits, aged twelve, sitting on a pony and clutching a silver cup to her chest; and beneath it the beginnings of an Airfix aeroplane she'd made, then abandoned. The box contained an endless assortment of juvenilia of a kind only interesting to a parent or a genealogist in years to come; but the thought that these items would in time secure Isabel a place among the ranks of the remembered, caught on my ribcage and tugged like a fish hook. It created a pain that was, by now, familiar. I put the lid back on the box but it made no difference. The pain stabbed on just the same.

My mother had said she found bonfires liberating. Bonfires were good. Bonfires allowed you to start afresh. She'd burnt all my Rupert Bear annuals — the things I was fond of. She carried them out in armfuls, even school library books I hadn't finished reading, and set fire to them with red diesel, too close to the woodshed where the kittens lived, so the black paint blistered on the corrugated iron sheets. The plastic covers produced a blue flame and a fume that gave you a sore throat if you breathed it in. The kind of flame you could look into and see yourself in. No sooner had the memory entered my head than there we were, Phileda and I, hauling stuff out of the attic to a place behind the beehives. And me saying, "See. What did I tell you? It's liberating, isn't it? It's time to start afresh."

And I'm screwing up the letters written with a scratchy pen. I'm making a nest out of some eighteenth-century rent rolls for the firelighters to sit in. I'm setting light to the corner of . . . words. I'm sending them back to dust, from before they became thought. It's after dinner and the grass is damp. There's a sweetness to the smoke; history smells wholesome, costly; must be its rarity value, as if we're burning a pyre of cobwebs. I'm piling on a collection of pressed

**129**

flowers that someone gathered a long time ago. They're brittle with age; the petals so fine they're like X-rays of petals; the colours so delicate they might have dissolved on someone's tongue, then been breathed out onto the page as vapour. There's a good blaze. Fragments of letters float upwards, touching the underside of the leaves on the apple tree. Words are all we have left to tell us we ever existed. Murder the words and history no longer exists. I've done something beyond myself and it's the sweetest drug.

Phileda's nodding, with a smudge across her nose, saying should we be doing . . .? But she's had so much to drink after so little dinner that her sentence trails off, as she's waylaid by the beauty of the flames. It's easy to get waylaid by the beauty of the flames and the way the smoke flowers upwards into patterns you could lay your head on. It's a beautiful night. I hand Phileda the box containing Isabel's childhood. She frowns when she sees what it contains and what I'm asking her to do. The chimneys of the house rise above the trees behind her and out of the top of her head like a pagan crown. She hesitates. She must not hesitate. I grasp her hand and for a second I lose all sense of sense. I begin to dance around the flames. She follows me. She thinks it's a game. I suppose it *is* a sort of game. A game of little Indians. I do a rain dance and she copies. We're jumping through and around the rising smoke and hooting with our hands pressed against our mouths. All the time she's hugging the box under her arm. For a second, I think I hear faint cries rising from the charred heap; it's the sound the dead would make if you wiped a gravestone clean. Her face is flushed with excitement and exertion. Then she remembers the box. She brings it out from under her arm and quickly tips its contents onto the fire. Swimming badges (fifty and one hundred metres), a small bear with button eyes, piano certificates (grades three and five) and the photographs of Isabel curling inside the flames. She looks to me for approval. I give it. The grey wings of an Airfix model begin to melt.

# CHAPTER
# EIGHT

Isabel came home at the beginning of the summer holiday. She brought Adrian with her. I watched them get out of his convertible. Adrian with his tiny blond curls and tweed jacket with elbow patches, just like she'd said. He rushed round to her side and opened the door. Then he stood and looked up at the house, running a hand through his hair to show he was surprised by the size of Critchley. Isabel laughed. She looked healthier, rounder and, if it was possible, prettier, as though his admiration was a soft cloth he'd polished her with. She linked his arm and I saw her pointing to where the formal garden had once been and to where there'd been an icehouse until it was blown up in the war by a stray bomb, and to where the foundations of the earlier house might have been. All the things I'd told her.

I knocked on the window and they both looked up. Isabel waved and screamed and pulled Adrian's sleeve in mock impatience to see me. A moment later we were colliding extravagantly on the stairs, our voices plaiting together as they'd done once before in the echo of the stairwell.

**132**

"This is my best friend," she said improbably to Adrian.

"I've heard a lot about you," he said, smiling and offering his hand to me.

"People still say that?" I said. He blushed. Easy as winding a piece of hair round my finger. "But it's nice to hear." His face relaxed. "Awful not to be talked about."

"Much worse," said Isabel. "Where's Mum?"

"Upstairs."

"I'll find her." She left us standing on the stairs. The scent of other places — same places, same food — on their clothes filling up the space; the whole atmosphere changed at once: luggage and carrier bags filling up the hallway, tennis rackets and spilling files, breaking in on the peace of the house.

"What a place!" He looked around him and then went to view a picture on the wall, a seascape with a battleship, in my opinion the most uninteresting picture in the house.

"Your line of work, I hear."

"Sailor? No. I'm an auctioneer." I didn't laugh. I thought how well he'd fit in at Critchley given half a chance. I offered to show him round the house. "Shouldn't we wait for Isabel?" he said.

"She won't mind. She's not that interested in history and, besides, she'll be ages with Phileda."

"OK, great," he said, smiling. "You lead the way." I showed him the ground floor first, explaining which parts of the building had been added at a later date: the pantries and the service rooms. I knew he'd love the gun room. It was a grown-up boy's den, full of dangerous toys and soft leather smells. I took out the key from a lidless teapot sitting on the shelf and unlocked the gun cabinet. He moved to the magnetic pull of Geoffrey's twelve-bores, his tongue protruding slightly from his mouth; his fingers reaching for the triggers and the barrels. "Fabulous," he cooed. "What an amazing collection." Then his eyes caught sight of the nets and rods standing to attention in a corner. "Do they have fishing?" he asked. And the use of that "they", denoting them and us, sent a tingle up my spine.

"They have six miles of the best fishing in the county," I said. He shook his head and laughed.

"I think I must have died and gone to heaven." I relocked the cupboard and we moved on to the main rooms. We went into the drawing room. The windows were open and the woozy, pink scent of old roses mingled with the aroma of wood-ash from the fireplace. A bee came in and out. "Rooms like this were built to be looked out of," he said, walking to the window.

"It's an English trait," I said. "The French laugh at our obsession with views. They can't understand why we look at the view first and then the room. They think we're primitive." He turned his back on the view and looked at the room.

"They have a point," he said. "This is magnificent. Is didn't tell me about any of this."

"No," I said, as we left the room. "I think it embarrasses her."

We did the other smaller rooms and then I took him to the kitchen — the only room that seemed appropriate to my station now Isabel was back. I made him tea. I gave him biscuits. I learned the details of his life and committed them to memory. We waited. He walked over to the fridge and made the word "fork" out of some abandoned magnetic letters. I asked him if he was nervous about meeting a future in-law. He said he hadn't thought about Isabel's friendship in those terms. But the words moved stubbornly out of his mouth, suggesting the contrary. Empty, predictable moments followed. A blue tit settled on a rope of nuts outside the window, exposing the white nut flesh through the red net. I wound an elastic band around the salt cellar until it snapped. Eventually, he asked me a question about myself. He asked me how I kept busy without Isabel. I told him that one of my favourite pastimes was to chop logs. But the level of satisfaction depended on the quality of the log.

I said: "Isn't it strange how when someone has been away for a long time and you've been left behind, you've got to learn to trust them all over again?"

"God, yes." His face came alive. "I used to feel like that when my mother came home, having been away for weeks on end. She expected me to love her straight away, like it was before she'd gone. But I couldn't." He stopped; surprised with himself, his face suddenly remote, tired, as though everything in his head was too heavy to carry. I looked through my eyelashes at him.

"Absence is the worst kind of betrayal."

He snorted a laugh. "So deep, so soon?"

"It's the country air — it focuses the mind." He bent his head and through his hair I could see the pinkness of his scalp, like a baby's. I tried to listen for sounds from upstairs but it was quiet, not even the creak of boards from Phileda's room.

I got up and filled the kettle. Then outside the door I heard footsteps move across the different floor finishes of the hallway: marble, wood and the muffled thud of leather soles on carpet. Adrian glanced at himself in the side of a copper pan, not minding that I saw. Then Isabel and Phileda entered the room, in a golden mist of Phileda's old perfume dating back to the days before Geoffrey left — Phileda no longer loose and floating, but Phileda back in chiffon and the armour of close-fitting cashmere; hair scalloped and helmet-stiff with spray. Phileda resurrected in the image of Phileda.

Dour, old Popey stood outside the window, smiling and waving his garden fork at Isabel. Miraculous that those fingers made things grow. They looked like slithers of horn closed around the stem of the fork. In order to wave back, Isabel had to unlink her hand from her mother's: unbuttoned, severed, she was free to throw her hand up in the air. Phileda grasped it again as soon as it came down, as though it was a bridal bouquet.

"Thrilled to meet you," said Phileda, descending upon Adrian like a cloud. "Really thrilled to meet you."

Isabel said, "Right, let's have some tea and I'll show you round the house."

Adrian started to speak. But I interrupted, kicking his sentence into the long grass, and said, "Yes,

Adrian's dying to see the house. He's talked of nothing else." He smiled foolishly at Isabel and then glanced at me, complicit.

"Of course, I'd love to see it," said Adrian. And we were suddenly conspirators, blooded by the lie.

That night Isabel asked me to sleep in her room like I used to. I said I would, but only for the night — I told her that once you'd become accustomed to luxury it was impossible to give it up; the green room had spoilt me. "I knew you'd get too grand for me in the end," she laughed, thinking I was joking.

She turned off the lamps. Two pinpricks of light from a distant car moved across the forehead of Kate Bush on the wall. She continued as though the darkness hadn't happened. "For a minute there, she had me worried. It really was quite spooky going in and finding her lying on the bed with all the curtains closed, and what *did* she think she was wearing?"

Isabel's words slid into the blackness like swimmers.

"You poor thing. What you've had to put up with! But it's OK now: I'm back. And you can see the difference in her already, can't you?"

Words, like pointed missiles sent to score.

"She and Adrian are getting on so well. Did you see them at lunch? He told me he really likes her. She's everything his mother wasn't. He said, 'At least she was there for you Isabel. You shouldn't be so hard on her.' "

Words like broken glass and skin meeting.

"He's right, I suppose. I know things haven't been so easy for her either. But it took *him* to point that out. It took *him* to make me realise how lucky I am. Makes you realise how much there is to unlearn about yourself. The other day we spent twenty minutes looking at a leaf together."

Words like a flesh wound, opened to receive salt.

"Can you imagine it? I've never wasted time like that. I've never stopped and actually looked at things before. He says the most obvious, simple, silly things, like the best things in life are free: but they take on new meaning when he says them. It's strange when everything that's been a joke suddenly becomes the most important thing in the world. He's taught me to listen and to hear, and to look and see, and I view the world in a new way now. I see Mum in a new way too. He says I'm spiritually so much older than her and it's the most helpful thing anyone's ever said to me. I feel closer to her now than I've ever felt."

Words like storm damage.

"Diane, are you asleep? Are you?"

"I have a plan," announced Isabel, the following morning. We were sitting round the breakfast table. Adrian was picking seeds out of a pomegranate with a compass. "I think we should go on a fishing expedition." Nobody answered. "Don't all shout at once," she said. "Come on, you two, what d'you think?" She reached across the table and flicked the side of my nose.

"Ouch, Isabel, that really hurt," I said.

"Sorry, Piglet, I just didn't think you were attending." Piglet was her new name for me. I felt the

138

pressure of it like a footprint on my chest; felt the weight of a new, confident Isabel striding over me.

"It's a brill idea though, don't you think?" She was in unusually high spirits.

"If you say so," I said, going back to a dot-to-dot puzzle on the back of the cereal packet.

"I'll get Mum and tell her to make us a picnic. In fact, she can come too. She needs an airing after being stuck in this house for so long."

Isabel jumped to her feet. I'd only reached number twelve of the puzzle and I knew it would come out in the shape of a horse with wings; there were stars in the background. I supposed it must be Pegasus.

Adrian said, "Isabel, eat these, there are fifty-two in all."

"You have them. I don't like pomegranates."

"But you told me you did."

"Did I? How amusing of me. I must have said it just to make myself sound more interesting."

Adrian tutted and pet-scolded like a besotted father. "Isn't she naughty?" he said to no one in particular. Isabel went to find Phileda. I didn't want to go fishing, but Isabel in the mood she was in meant there would be no getting out of it. An hour later we were standing outside Critchley with fishing rods, nets and an array of wicker baskets waiting to be loaded into the car.

Phileda appeared in a floppy white hat and white shoes, proffering midge cream, saying: "It's not a big picnic — just a few hors d'oeuvres to keep us going." Adrian put the roof down on his car.

Isabel was the last to emerge. She came out empty-handed and said, "Right, are we ready then? Great. Then let's go."

We drove down lanes I'd never been on before. They were private to the Critchley estate, sandy tracks made by farm vehicles; the bottom of Adrian's car brushed on the centre green. Through the trees the river flashed past, silver. Soon we arrived at a clearing. "Here, here," screamed Phileda.

"No, don't be mental, Mum, it's further on," said Isabel. A could of dust rose behind the car. Eventually we pulled in near a break in a hedge. "This is it," said Isabel. "Park here." It was cool in the shade of the trees.

"The de Burghs have always fished this river," Phileda told Adrian on the way down to the water's edge. "It's quite historic really. There are photos in the gun room of them picnicking here and the stuffed trout on the wall . . . that was caught on a line from this bank." She took his arm and he steered her round the tree roots. "It's good to have a man about," she said, patting his wrist. Isabel ran ahead and I carried the fishing rods.

There was rapid movement on the banks: small, watery creatures darting for the cover of the foliage. Willows, like the fingers of love-sick girls, trailed their branches in the water. We laid out rugs and unpacked the picnic. Adrian assembled the rods. A dragonfly hummed across the water. Isabel rummaged in a basket. "Mum, this is a rubbish picnic. Why didn't you let Piglet help you?"

"Darling, that's not a very kind name for Diane."

"Oh, I think it suits her. Look at that little piggy nose, the way it turns up at the end."

I ignored her; heard the water moving over stones, felt its quiet power. Adrian said that if we didn't be quiet we'd scare away the fish.

"Wait," said Isabel, jumping to her feet. "The picture's not complete," and she pulled a khaki hat from her pocket that was smocked with flies and hooks. She placed it on Adrian's head. "It was Dad's," she said to Phileda. "Look, it fits perfectly." Phileda looked away.

"Come on, you," said Adrian, picking up a rod. "I'm going to show you how to fish."

"I know how to fish."

"No you don't, not properly. Let's see you in action." They walked away from the trees and went to the water's edge. Isabel took the rod in her right hand and the line in her left. She cast and cast again. The line snaked above their heads. "Not bad," said Adrian. "But try and feel the line beneath your fingers." They moved further into the bend of the river, almost out of sight. "Like this." He put his arms round her; draped himself around her like a cloak. And they cast together, both hands on the rod.

Phileda was engrossed in cutting bread. I picked up a spare rod and went to the water's edge. I could see the two of them standing together in the river, Adrian's cheek tight against hers. He scraped her hair back behind her ear and kissed her, and she appeared not to notice. She seemed not to notice the closeness of another person, as though being loved was an ordinary experience, something you took for granted because it had always been so. The water had darkened the legs of their jeans. Adrian's were rolled up to the knee and the down on his calves was also dark, like rain that had rolled off the roofs of farm buildings. Bright pinpricks of light glistened on the surface of the water.

The rod was in my hand. I was thinking of catches and what bait it would take to hook a prize of human proportions. I cast my rod towards them. I had a sense of being in an empty church with voodoo going on; there were dark spells and mischief afoot in the greening river light. The hook span through the air. It turned and pirouetted like a magnet on the draw and, by some miracle of circumstance, landed on Adrian's hat. The line went taut in my hands and as I pulled, the hat came too. They jumped apart. Adrian standing in the river with his trousers rolled up, touching his head in disbelief: the ladder-smacking joke of it. Isabel began to laugh.

"My God, Diane, you could have had my eye out," yelped Adrian.

"What an incredible shot," said Isabel, gulping down laughter.

"Incredible," I breathed to myself. Then in a louder voice: "Adrian, I'm so sorry. I'm useless at fishing. The line just went the other way." A prickling sensation spread across the back of my neck. The coincidence of my crack shot filled me with a new fuel. It was proof that something must be done. I would espalier the future. I would train its boughs to form a pattern to my liking.

142

"What a shot," said Isabel again, this time shaking her head. "You've got a rival, Adrian. Someone who can fish as well as you." Even Phileda laughed. And two ducks lifted from the reed beds.

The tumble of that afternoon. We caught no fish that day.

The following day they went out. Isabel offered to stay behind and cook lunch, which was her way of asking me to stay behind and cook lunch. Without looking at me Phileda said, "You are a dear, Diane," then slid behind Isabel, using her like a shield, embarrassed, perhaps, that she had once called me Amelia.

Isabel wanted to show Adrian St Mary's, where ranks of ancient de Burghs lay rigored in sepulchral splendour: a stone church on the corner of two connecting roads, where yew trees ensured no light ever illuminated the stained glass. Gravel hit the underside of the car as it moved away down the drive.

I went upstairs and lay down. I thought about the time my mother had tied a soft woollen scarf under my chin, before leaving me late for lessons in the carpark of a new school. She'd leant over and drawn an index finger down my nose. She'd said, "You do as I say, not as I do, and you won't end up in the stew." It's what she always said when there was something ahead neither of us wanted to face. I got up. Alone, I moved through the house as though it was a waiting room. I opened magazines, then closed them again. I went into the old housekeeper's room where the wooden draining board was white from lack of use. I picked at a patch of flaking paint round the light switch until it resembled a roan horse in the pinkness of the plaster beneath. I went into Isabel's room and touched the labels of sweaters that were strewn inside out across the backs of chairs.

I took Phileda's quilted jacket off a peg in the cloakroom and went for a walk in it in the garden. In the shadow of a magnolia tree I sought out the consolation of its pockets. My fingers closed around some loose change and a tissue. I took the tissue out and lifted it to my nose. The distinguishable components were face powder, nail varnish and whisky. There was even some lipstick on a corner. I wondered how a pink smudge on a tissue could actually cause physical pain; how much I missed Phileda now Isabel was back. I wondered what I would make happen on account of it. The poplars whispered conspiratorially near the boundary wall. It had turned into another beautiful day but there were no clouds. Skies were boring without the animation of clouds.

When they returned Adrian seemed subdued, like someone who hadn't entirely got the joke but laughed anyway. Phileda looked happy, her smile unravelling into a grin like a pulled ribbon on a gift, for no reason other than that Isabel looked at her. She said, "Dash it all. Let's celebrate and have some champagne."

But Isabel wagged her finger: "Remember what we talked about earlier?"

Phileda crossed her legs: "Of course, darling. I just thought . . ." Isabel went over and kissed the top of her head.

"*Just* thoughts are very bad for you, you know."

Dinner passed in a sop of glazed pork and red cabbage. The candles in their silver sticks burned without flickering. No one minded that I got up after each course to clear the plates away. They sat and continued their talk about various de Burgh ancestors: the one who'd lost the tip of his nose at Waterloo; the other who'd been saved by a cigar case at Sebastopol. For whatever reason, Isabel was trying to out-ace Adrian on the issue of family history. Throwing her arms apart, she said, "Sorry, Diane, this must be very boring for you." It was the first time Isabel had used hand signals to indicate the gulf between us. The taste of anger in my mouth was suddenly exact, metallic, like blood spilling in from a cut lip.

In a voice separate from myself I said, "I just can't understand why you find the dead so interesting. I mean, let's talk about something real, something that's happened. What's the very first thing you remember?" I told them that my first memory was of the outdoors and that the outdoors was where I belonged. It was a time when I seemed only to recognise things with my teeth and nails. I remembered all the colours of the fields and the ripped-off wing of a rook resting against a limestone boulder, and what happened to a bale of hay when it became saturated with rain and the way pebbles looked in the shallow part of the river. No one had ever seen such exchanges of colour. These were the meaningful things; the things that really mattered, the things that forced you to give way to life, weren't they?

No one answered. They just sat and looked at me with their lips slightly apart until Adrian said, "That's beautiful, Diane." It was beautiful because I'd made it up, like art. Lies were more beautiful than truth. Lies were hatched; they slept in eggs like tiny serpents, waiting to be born blinking into the light. Truth, on the other hand, was a blunt line drawn with a marker pen on a white wall. When you swallowed truth, it stuck in the throat like a fur ball.

"But I wasn't just talking about the dead," broke in Isabel, ignoring all I'd said. "It's about how I fit into it all." Adrian kept his eyes on me for longer than was polite. My anger gave way to pity, then to conceit, then to contempt; but in the end these feelings returned again to pity — pity for Isabel, because I knew if I shook her hard enough, she would drop into my lap like a piece of fruit and the pips of her were already visible beneath her pearly-white skin; ripe. "It's our family history that makes us what we are," she went on, turning to Adrian. "When I show you the papers in the attic tomorrow, you'll see what I mean."

Silence fell across the table. Silence like after a snowfall; the same silence you find in a conifer plantation where nothing lives, only disembodied eyes watch. Phileda's beads fell against the edge of her desert plate as she pushed her chair back from the table. I didn't lift my face to meet hers because I knew she wanted me to. Phileda who'd been mine, but was now not mine. I knew she was thinking of the flames and whether it was possible to cancel out time or recreate matter out of ashes. Isabel's words had wiped the lipstick off the evening. This, I would remember, was the moment when everything began to slip so perfectly into one; the moment when the shape of what I would make happen emerged before me, whole and fully formed. The clock struck eleven. Phileda said goodnight, then wandered from the room like a lost tourist. I helped myself to some more pudding. Adrian ran his finger round the rim of his glass but no tune would come.

Later, when Phileda knocked on the door, I was lying on the bed thinking of the very first thing I'd bought. The very first time I'd had money in my hand. It was a note — five-pound notes were larger then, less apologetic; proper money. I bought chocolate. I didn't want chocolate but I bought it anyway. I handed the money over to the woman behind the counter. There were rows of sweets in glass jars behind her head. The shop smelt of newspapers and sugar. Then I must have fallen asleep, and for half a second I was dreaming I didn't like chocolate and actually I didn't like being a child any more. And the relief was like a dam wall breaking when I woke and found myself inside the zipped-up skin of an adult, lying among the silk hangings and the full-length mirrors of the green room.

I got off the bed and opened the door. Phileda was standing there, wearing an extravagantly thin garment with roses printed over it. Her eyes were red as though a sun had gone down behind them. I brought her into the room and then stepped out onto the landing to make sure no one had followed her, as they did in "The

Third Man", or was it "Casablanca"? Over and over she said, "We're in a fix, we're in a fix."

It was raining outside: thin, night rain scented with fresh air. The gutter outside the window gurgled gently like a happy baby.

"You're not in a fix," I assured her. "They're only papers and a few other things. Not the end of the world."

"The end of the world," she repeated blankly, as though it really was. "I don't want to hurt Isabel," she said.

Three thoughts assailed me at the same time: the first, that I would never trust her again; the second, how good-looking she must have been once; and the third, that now she'd have to live with the consequences of choosing Isabel over me.

She played with her beads, gathered them up, then let them drop. I told her I'd sort the whole thing out with Isabel. If she liked, I'd tell her it was my fault; that I'd burned the papers. I'd tell her I was just trying to be helpful. She didn't say, "No don't." She didn't say, "Now, darling, I couldn't have you do that, it's just too self-sacrificing." No, she didn't say that. She said, "Oh, would you, *would you?*" and then she fell into my unwilling arms and laid her head on my shoulder, as though it was all she had to do to make everything right.

# CHAPTER
# NINE

Nothing happened the day after or the day after that. The weather was too hot for action. The rain had cleared the clouds and the sun burned, burned the gravel until it was too hot to walk on with bare feet. Burned the iron roofs of the potting sheds until the paint shrank. Heat ripples rose off the earth. Record-breaking temperatures the news said: the reservoirs were low; the weatherman urged everyone to put a brick in the cistern to save water, not to wash the car or use a hosepipe. Phileda kept the lawn sprinklers on. The crack of ice cubes shrinking in warm drinks. The things I remember: Isabel sliding into the fountain basin, saying to Adrian, "Come on in, the water's lovely," her arms stretched round the edge of the granite bowl like white strips of cotton. The trees were still, perfectly still, not even a shimmer.

I watched, unseen, from an upstairs window. She pushed a weed-covered toe towards him through the water. He crouched by the edge of the fountain, tried to catch it, thighs as thick as trees in his tight trousers and every muscle delineated like a life class. His white shirt was open at the neck. He'd caught the sun, his hair had paled almost to white, like a child's. I leaned against the glass trying to make something human of its flatness, but it would give me nothing, nothing except a veil of my own breath. The foot disappeared into the water. She was wearing a black swimsuit. Everything within the lens of my seeing seemed either black or white; there were no greys or suggestions of other colours. She dropped her body beneath the water so only her head was visible. In the centre of the fountain, a fat lead cherub stood on one foot and urinated into the water — high culture and low humour rolled into one. Isabel moved round the side of the fountain like a spoon round a bowl. She faced the cherub. She let the back of her hand play in the arc of water that streamed from him. She didn't take her gaze off Adrian; her eyes were like a clever trick with paint, the eyes of a portrait, stalking. Then in a movement that was utterly adult, utterly meaningful, she slowly parted her lips and took the arc of water that emanated from between the cherub's thighs into her mouth. And she took it lovingly, with feeling, with a movement of the lips that was akin to the eating of ripe cherries. Adrian sat there like an animal transfixed by the gaze of a predator. He read it as a sign, as a waving flag; as a promise. From the edge of the fountain he reached out towards her, but she moved away like a shy fish and, laughing now, pretended to cough and splutter, pretended to choke. Her chasteness was a vault to which she voluntarily retreated. He hit the water with his hand.

"Poor Adrian," I whispered to the glass. "Brave little man."

★ ★ ★

The things I remember: walking towards the apple room with the sun on our backs, the smell of his leather jacket softening in the heat. The things we said. *Numero uno.* Plastic is the skin of the modern world. Where there's a will, there's money. Did your sister leave teeth marks when she did that? Listen, listen, here's one for you. That's so unfunny. Time travelling down the twist of an elastic band as he tried to explain the universe to me. Five different conversations in the space of five minutes. We talked as we walked in and out of the shade of the copper beech, and the horses stood by the gate that led into the park with their lower lips dangling so flies crawled in and out.

Phileda and Isabel had gone out for the afternoon insisting that dinner was their affair. They'd left me standing in the kitchen wondering at the skill they had for glamourising the mundane: how the procuring of dinner could be turned into an edifying pursuit that would both educate and amuse, and later provide stories to last the whole evening through. A foray into the outside world was like a trip to the funfair for them.

Isabel had forgotten about the attic. "Do something cool," she said to me, "let Adrian cast his auctioneer's eye over the outbuildings. A Rembrandt is the very least he can find for us."

So there we were, walking towards the apple room with the sun on our backs. Everything secure and square and thought through. The courtyard with its cobbled ground sloping towards a drain in the middle where they used to wash the carriages; cobwebs spandrelling the windows of the buildings like sleep in eyes. The stairs were narrow, not painted but grimy pine-coloured. It was dark after the sunshine. Adrian was behind me. So close I could have kicked his chin with my heels. "You go first," I said.

"OK. Mind out," and the clothes on our stomachs touched as he slid past me on the stairs. The room was small, as though it had been designed as a joke for a children's tea party; a kitten-jumble of junk and dust: loops of baling twine and horsehair tufts protruding from ripped mattresses; chicken wire covering the windows. There was a swallow's nest attached to a corner of the ceiling, with a crust of droppings beneath it on the floor: flecks of mauve, black and buff. The bird's tail forked out of the nest. "A second clutch," said Adrian. He moved into the room, scratched the side of his nose, marvelling at the potential of the mess on the floor; the secrets it might harbour.

I asked him, could he believe it? Could he believe what some people would discard? He said, "Different ways of seeing," and then began rummaging. His fingers like insects running over dusty surfaces. The smell of warm apples rose from beneath a bed of straw. He moved across the room, stooping so as not to hit his head on the sloping eaves. He fitted handles onto broken teacups, turned the wicks up on rusty lamps, and I wondered how I could make myself want him enough to do what I had to do: the leather smell of him and his yellow teeth, big and suitable for a mouth like that; his hand as he raised it to his face like a goal, something you would kick a ball into. I stood behind him, willing him with unmoving hands towards a pile of pictures, some with broken frames, others with no glass at all stacked against the wall. He moved towards them, as I knew he would, because leaning pictures had that appeal: that might-be, could-be, anything's-possible appeal. He flicked through the stack. A small gilt rosette broke off a frame, leaving a gash in the gesso beneath. He picked it up and placed it carefully on the windowsill, which made me laugh because so much of the rest of it was missing.

He came to the back of the pile, near where the plaster was coming off the wall. I talked because I didn't want him to know I was expecting him to find what I knew he would find. I talked about the pile of newspapers I'd found on the floor from 1945, wondering what was happening in the world then, telling him how different it all must have been. It was the end of the war, wasn't it? There was bunting in the streets and everyone ate jelly. What else, I asked? What else was happening in 1945? But he didn't answer. He'd pulled out a smallish picture and was staring at it as though it was a swinging watch in front of his eyes. His face had reddened as I knew it would, his eyes grew wider.

"What?" I said, moving close to him. "What's that you've found?"

"No," he said, "it can't be. Why's this here? This shouldn't be up here."

"Show me," I said, pulling his arm. It was the Cooper I'd taken off the wall of the drawing room barely an hour ago. The Cooper I knew he hadn't seen.

The tiny painting the firemen had been told to rescue first if the house was on fire.

"Is it something good?" I asked.

"It's more than good." He turned it backwards, forwards, searching for clues to confirm his disbelief. "D'you see those cuffs? How they're whacked in with one bold stroke of the brush? Those ringlets — look — bang, bang, bang," swiping an imaginary paintbrush, criss-cross, through the air. "It's vintage Samuel Cooper. My God, do you know, I think it's right."

"Incredible," I said. "It's amazing what people chuck out." I went back to sorting through the papers. "Nineteen forty-five. What else were people doing in nineteen forty-five except curling their eyelashes and doing *trompe l'oeil* on their legs with gravy browning?"

"No, you don't understand. Listen, this is worth a lot of money. This is the art find of the century. And I've found it. Me. Here. In this apple room. I've found it. My God. Wait till Isabel hears."

*Is a bell. Dis abel.* Making it easy for me. Making two forks of a river run into one. Turning matter into compost beneath the surface. Isabel who didn't know what the capital of Poland was, but who knew the difference between humus and humous; one you forked in, the other you ate, she'd said.

"Let's not tell Isabel yet. If you say it's a Cooper we could go to the library and find out about him. She won't believe us otherwise. If we tell her we found it in the apple room, she'll say it must have been thrown out for a reason. The reason being it's a worthless fake."

154

"This is no fake," said Adrian, tearing the brown paper off the back of the frame. A wasp flew in through the chicken wire; he didn't wave it away. He let it buzz round his head and hands as though his good fortune had made him impervious to stings, nature's worst. "But you're right. We'll wait," he said, then laid the picture to one side. He got up off the floor, forgetting to brush the dust from his knees, his face bursting into smiles.

"Wait till she hears," he said, and began dancing round the room. "Wait till she hears." He grasped my hands, urged me to move with him, to share his delight. I took his hands and like two sycamore seeds floating down to earth we seemed to spin in the air. I knew what would happen off by heart, not the details — the hows and the eventual wherefores — but the moment our lips would meet, how he would taste and the eventual pulling away. I reminded myself of the consequences which acted as a sighting shot, keeping the end in mind. We stopped dancing but not abruptly. His pleasure at finding the picture manifested itself in a single kiss delivered to my cheek with the dry chastity of a choir boy. But another was to come. I pulled him via the corners of his jacket towards me; kissed him again and this time on the lips. I had the insane image of two plungers meeting, of an unblocking taking place. Hands, arms and wrung skin, there was an urgency, a need in him to go further. He hooked his hand over my ear and under my hair. Kissed me again, harder. Then came the inevitable breaking away as conscience took hold: the feeling that we were a dark liquid spill and that no matter how much mopping up took place there would always be a stain.

# CHAPTER
# TEN

The heat, not as sharp, not as intense as it had been, but the sense of hot ash raining down all the same. The stones of the house connecting with other stones and growing warm through the day, then turning cold again by morning. The curtains remained closed so as to prevent bleaching of the furniture. Four large leaves from the tulip tree on the lawn, the heat getting to us all, even to nature.

Isabel and I went up onto the roof of the breakfast room to sunbathe. It was a flat lead roof. We took towels, bowls of popcorn, drinks with straws; our books for show. We lay on inflatable mattresses, she in a bikini, me in a swimsuit, and talked. We talked about how lucky she was to have found Adrian. What it meant. The beautiful children that would be created from their union and the union itself. I turned my face away from her towards the horizon, where a jet had made a line in the clouds above the hills; I said yes, they'd have curls, beautiful golden curls that would sit on their heads like the waves that floated across rock pools until Phileda stroked them flat.

"I want it to happen," she said, propping herself up on her elbows. "He's made up for Dad." Her legs were

**157**

the colour of dough, something to be worked between finger and thumb. "I ache for him. But everything's better if you wait for it. It's best to keep men waiting. Love must come before lust. But that's not to say I can't tease him a little in the meantime." She rolled over onto her stomach and laughed, and asked me to unhook her. "Ouch, your fingers are cold." The catch of her bikini had imprinted the initial N on her back.

Old Popey was moving around in the shrubbery below. It was as if he could smell her, as though she were exuding ripples of oestrogen, or whatever it was that made men arrive at women's feet like letters to be picked up and discarded at will. He started to whistle a tune: "If I was the only boy in the world and you were the only girl". The old pervert with tinned peaches on his mind, licking his lips and drooling over Isabel. I felt the urge to put him out of his misery as though he were an injured animal, to kosh him, to do what birds did to defective chicks, to crush him.

Isabel put a finger to her lips and slid on her stomach towards the balustrade. She looked down, then picked up a wrappered sweet, a caramel, and threw it between the pillars at him. "Miss Isabel, what you doing up there?" came his voice from below. She ducked down and put her hand over her mouth to suppress giggles.

"That's funny," I said, "but it's not as funny as this." I picked up the box of sweets and hurled the whole thing off the side of the roof.

"Hey, what's that you're up to now?" shouted Popey, to the sound of sweets raining down on his head.

"You're mad, you know that?" said Isabel, doubled up with laughter.

"Or this," I said, picking up the earthenware bowl that contained the popcorn and throwing that too. There was an eerie silence as the bowl hung in the air. And then came the thud and the howl, and the inevitable clicking apart of the earthenware as it bounced off Popey onto the ground.

"Fucking mad," said Isabel, suddenly not laughing any more. She sat up, corralling her breasts back into the cups of her bikini. "You've really hurt him."

"Serves him right," I said, "for sniffing around like that." We looked over the balustrade and Popey was hurrying away clutching his arm and moaning like a lost calf.

"Poor Popey," said Isabel.

"That halo of yours will slip and strangle you one of these days, Is," I said. "His mother should never have taken her foot off his head."

"You're all heart, you," she said, embarrassed now and laughing to hide her embarrassment. When Popey reached the beech tree, he turned back and shook his fist at us.

"You're in trouble now, Is," I said. And meant it.

We met Adrian on the way down. He told us he was about to shut the windows; there was a storm on the way. Isabel linked her arms round his neck and kissed him. "Am I gorgeous, or am I gorgeous?" she said.

"You're gorgeous," Adrian said quickly. He ran his hands down her sides. She pulled away.

"I'm hot and sticky. I'm going for a shower."

My toes sank into the bristly pelt of a wild animal on the floor. She left us standing together, looking everywhere except at each other. I made a half-hearted attempt to cover myself by throwing a towel over my shoulder. I said, "Look, about the kiss, about yesterday." He broke in and said he was sorry. How he was excited, happy at finding the picture. How it seemed the obvious way to express himself. But how he felt stupid, like a puppy that had just peed on the carpet.

"Pact," I said. "It never happened, OK?" He hugged me like a brother. "The picture's safe. It's in your room, second drawer down. A week from now we'll tell them."

The storm didn't break for another three days in which time I surprised myself by catching a cold. I was grateful for it in a way. The vulnerability of the sick was a useful disguise. I wore it with panache. My adenoidal croon wrung sympathy from everyone. The phlegmy crackle in the throat; the cough you dug for and brought up and held in the mouth like the outer casing of frogspawn.

Phileda ordered me to bed, said, "Poor darling," then forgot about me. How little it mattered now. Events were in motion, the sense of rolling, aim straight, with skittles waiting at the end. Soon she would have no choice but to love me. I lay back on a cloud of pillows and enjoyed my cold. Adrian visited me frequently; Isabel less. He brought me trays of food, each with a different-coloured rose in a china teacup, and

**160**

sometimes a date or a tangerine or a honeyed drink, for strength. I would pat the edge of the bed and he would sit. I would wait for best impact before blowing my nose, until my head filled with mucus. The blow rumbling through my nostrils and into the tissue, captured, an aborted egg without its shell. And he would put his hand to my forehead, check my pulse, the risen glands in my neck — just to touch, just to connect himself with another living body.

Once, he came wearing nothing on his feet and we lay on the bed like new shoes packed in a shoe-shop box, feet to face. I said, "Close your eyes and see if you can stand this?" and I took out a biro and drew a figure of eight on the bottom of his foot, expecting him to recoil instantly. But he barely moved. He just lay there with the look of an archangel on his face. I went on drawing, turning the figure of eight into a parody of a woman by blacking the teeth and putting stubble on the chin, and wrote "Isabel" underneath, just to see where we'd got to; how far we'd come. He awoke from his trance, smiling, and his first impulse was to try to touch me again. He grabbed my wrist and took the pen from my hand, and turned his foot upside down to look.

"Yes, I can certainly see a resemblance," he said, "except in the nose. The nose should be bigger." And he put on his cutest look, the one his mother had told him to hold for the camera. And I knew I wasn't supposed to think how disloyal he'd been by saying that, but how cute he was instead, how cute and how witty, and how blameless he was; a boy worth knowing.

The male of the species would do anything to further their own cause, unlike the female who did it because it fed the darkest part of the soul.

When he was least expecting it, I asked him if he'd noticed a change in Isabel, slipping the sentence in like money in a slot, paying in to get something out. Didn't he think she was distant, a little removed from the world around her? And could I tell him something in confidence? (My voice sounding reasonable, calm, concerned.) I could? Well, the other day she threw a bowl at Popey for no reason at all. She threw it off the roof and it hit him on the arm hurting him badly. To be quite frank, it had frightened me a little. It was so unprovoked, so pointless. What was the matter? What was the cause of her anger?

With a dry note of sadness in his voice he said, "I don't know. I can't get close enough to ask."

I aired the hypothesis that perhaps it was me. That I was the stick that stirred the rubbish up in everyone.

"Oh no, no. Don't think like that. Isabel needs you." He touched the top of my toes, one by one, and I knew he was counting each little piggy to market in his head. A breeze came in through the window, carrying on it diesel fumes but not the sound of an engine.

"Perhaps I should leave." And with those words came a slide show of images of The Shack on the Lower Road: cups of tea with meals, bread and butter with everything, the memory that no one had been in the audience to watch me in nativity plays. There was nothing in the world that would make me leave Critchley now: earthquake, flood or plague.

"If you go, the whole house collapses," he said.

When the storm came I was ready for it. I was out of bed, sitting on the windowsill of the green room and wondering what it would be like to travel through the gut of another person. Clouds as dark as cinders had closed in on the world. The sky was quiet; no birdsong, only the tambourine shush of a breeze going through the ash trees. The bare soil in the flowerbeds was already moist in anticipation of being serviced by the rain; the plants were alert, ready, the expression of drought gone from their bell-like faces. Then it began, big drops of rain that sat on the surface of things and remained separate from the dust. From the window I watched it fall on the faux-leather roof of Adrian's car, the moment of freeze-frame when each drop hit the surface and rose up at the edge to form a watery crown. The drift of rain, landing on the ground in backward ticks, abundant and pleased with its own ferocity. Before long it had made new mini-maps in the earth, cut rivulets that swelled into rivers, forged contours where none were before, and gradually the bases of trees grew darker than the tops. It was beautiful to watch: seeing the world as though through tears.

I prepared for what I knew must come: shook the pillows and smoothed down the bedclothes. The first fork of lightning lit up the room. It hung in the violet sky like fingers waiting to be thrust into the eyes of a serpent. I counted one, two, three, four, then the thunder clapped the lightning an encore. The pleasure of being drowned out by sound, the biggest sound nature could make. The rain was a white sheet in front of the window and soon there was no distinction between land and sky.

Isabel burst into the room, nonchalant about the storm, but I could tell, nervous underneath.

"Better, are you?"

"Much, thanks."

"Mum's in bed. She hates storms. She had a bad time in Marrakesh once."

"I know," I said, remembering how she'd told me the story in Venice, touching my hand across the restaurant table and beginning, "You're the only one I've ever told," because of the reference to hashish. "I was young then," she'd said, looking into the wistful distance. And for once I didn't mock her vulnerability, not even to myself. I'd poured her more wine and offered her the bread sticks, warm in the knowledge that a shared confidence was a form of bondage and the breaking of bread only added to the sanctity of the moment. *You're the only one I've ever told*. And I believed it. Later, my heart beat so fast it kept me awake. It was the night she'd given me the necklace, slipping it off her own neck and placing it round mine: the reason being it was something of her own, unconnected to Geoffrey. Other things too: stopping alongside the Grand Canal so she could rub my hands in hers because they were cold; presenting an eyelash to me on the tip of her finger, having removed it from my eye. The sense that we were at the beginning of a story, when really we were at the end.

My hand slipped beneath my collar and sought out the chain. It was old and thin enough to adhere to the hollows of my neck. A small opal pendant hung from it. My fist closed around it and pulled. As it broke, it made a soft metallic sound like a press stud closing. Behind me, Isabel was saying how bored she was with the weather: couldn't go out, couldn't ride, couldn't do anything except yawn and grow fatter. She threw herself backwards onto the bed and the bedclothes closed around her face like water round a pebble. I let the chain drop into my shirt and went to the window. No view of any sort, only shapes, the world a rheumy mixture of glass and water.

"I've got an idea," I said. "Let's finish what your mother started in the attic."

"What did she start?" Isabel said, on the way up the stairs.

"She was sorting through boxes. Tidying up." I tried to keep what I knew off my face by thinking that outside the leaves would be dripping, dripping to a point and then springing up when the drip fell and returned to the earth. Isabel's step quickened. She threw open the door and a little breath of surprise escaped from her when she saw that the attic room was almost empty.

"Where's my stuff gone?" She said it so mildly that I thought my plan had failed even before it had got off the ground; a bird with a broken wing trying to take flight. She ran to the one remaining box, which was filled full of unfinished samplers for church hassocks and designs still on squared paper of lambs, lilies and crosses. She began to rummage with quick movements of both hands.

"I couldn't bear it," she was saying, "if anything's happened ..." the first notes of panic rising in her voice. Her skin was white, cold-seeming, and I thought of the bird lifting off the ground, its wings dark against the sun. "Where's my stuff?"

"Is. Don't be mad. Your mother had a bonfire, that's all. She asked me to help. Look, at least you can move in here now." I threw out my arms and pirouetted in the empty space.

She said, "What?" as if she'd heard the words but didn't understand them.

I noticed her mouth, as though for the first time. It was like a tight little shell, the twist getting tighter at the top. Her anger was suddenly metal-cold, calm almost, but with her eyes she threw knives.

"She did what?" My fingers were in the air, moving through the room. I watched them: the cut of a shark's fin through water, and for a moment I wished I could join Isabel in her rage, for the relief of it, like tearing up a thousand paper fines in one go.

When I looked again, Isabel was already halfway out of the door. In the stairwell she said, "You don't understand. How could you understand?" More half-words and a sob almost hidden by a burst of

**166**

thunder as she ran down the stairs. I closed my eyes and was filled with a terrible happiness.

I went back to my bedroom and waited.

Everything seemed sharper somehow. The blue flowers on the Edwardian washbowl, bluer; the mirror I pressed my hand to above the fireplace, colder. Cracks in the ceiling I'd never noticed before, but could see now as though they were fishermen's nets, sea-darkened, against the white. How a hunter feels, I thought, like a newly sharpened pencil, ready and alert. From the window I could pick out the small birds in the trees in spite of the rain, each one fluffing out their feathers in turn. I could hear Adrian's voice at the door, heavy and flat. He was asking to be let in against a background of other voices: Isabel's and Phileda's. They were shouting at each other. I checked myself in the mirror and in a rush of tenderness for myself, I saw in the lines around my eyes, how life had pummelled every bit of softness out of me. Adrian knocked again. The hunter who faced me in the mirror, knelt down and imagined he scooped up a handful of soil and pressed it to his nose, crumbled it, then smelled the air. "Come in," I said, ready.

In the room, his eyes stood out like two exclamation marks, his eyebrows raised above two dark spots. I asked him if he'd teach me how to play the piano; that I'd always wanted to learn.

"But I don't play the piano," he said, confused.

"I know," I said, "but we can learn together," and I laughed, ignoring the raised voices downstairs in the hallway; the voices with no objects to absorb them, only the flat walls making them louder. The windows of my room were steaming up and barely a breath released. The rain was slowing.

"No, I didn't come to talk about pianos." There was something disconnected in the way he spoke, like a metal link that had stretched too far. "They're having a big fight downstairs." He said they were like two angry bees and he didn't know what to do, had never seen Isabel so angry; what had got into her? Blaming her mother for burning her stuff. What kind of stuff, crown jewels? Without thinking he walked over to the mantelpiece, picked up a cup and turned it over, checking the maker's mark. But it didn't seem to register. He returned it to its saucer.

"With fighting dogs, the best thing to do is to throw something over them," I said.

"What d'you suggest? I go down with a blanket?"

"Well, I think you should go down, at least to referee. Their fights have a way of turning nasty. Best to put yourself between them."

He gave me a quick, anxious smile, of a kind a son gives his mother when trying to cover up a guilty act, and went downstairs. I checked my face in the mirror again and went out into the hallway to listen. I was wearing the wrong shirt; it was one size too small because it was Isabel's and the seams strained. My skin felt warm through it, like the overstuffed filling of a pie.

Phileda was whimpering and trying to talk at the bottom of the stairs; she threw out four words for sorry like a rope bridge towards Isabel. But none would

**168**

hook. Isabel's words, in contrast, volleyed up the stairwell. I warmed my hands in the heat of them. Then Phileda, in a slightly strangled voice, said: "Diane made me do it." There was an ominous pause.

"What the *fucking* hell d'you mean by that?" said Isabel. Phileda gasped. "That's just typical of you to blame someone else. Did you or did you not take my private property from the attic and burn it? It's a simple question, answer in your own time."

"Well, I did and I didn't."

"That's just so *horrible*," screamed Isabel. "Blaming it on someone else is worse than having done it in the first place."

"Darling."

"Don't darling me." Her anger moving towards violence. "You're weird, Mum. You know that? Fucking weird. How could you do something so obviously cruel? You, and only you, know why this hurts so much."

I looked down upon them and all I could see were the tops of their heads and the occasional thrown-out arm as they danced to the puppet-master's commands. Phileda supported herself against a console table, her hand caressing a gilded swan's head as though hoping to induce magic, to call down a black power. Adrian, at this point, tried to intercept with his palms turned to the floor in the manner of a policeman slowing traffic. Isabel misunderstood his meaning. He jarred with the flow of things, like a comma in the wrong place. With the imprecise logic of the vexed female she questioned his allegiance.

**169**

"Why are you sticking up for her? Whose side are you on, anyway?"

"No, Isabel, no. You're quite wrong. It's not about taking sides. It's about keeping things in perspective."

"And what would you know about keeping things in perspective? What's ever happened to you in your Mickey Mouse life that's been worth keeping in perspective?" In each of the four gilt mirrors I could see her. She looked like a small, proud queen all in black, with the rolled collar of her jersey rising high on her neck.

"You're just the same, Adrian," she wailed, moving towards the front door. "Diane where are you?"

I darted back into my room and quietly closed the door. The front door banged shut and I heard footsteps on the gravel as Isabel walked out into the warm rain still calling my name.

Adrian ran up the stairs and let himself into my room saying, "There's no sense in it. No sense." A song without a tune, just words, but music to my ears nevertheless.

While he described the scene downstairs, I washed my hands in the basin and dried them on a linen napkin. The washer inside the tap had withered. Metal turned against metal when I closed it; hard, nothing to soften it. There was a brown stain on the sink where the tap had dripped. A marginally disreputable stain like a yellow moustache. But the washbasin had been new once. I imagined the blue-white porcelain and the shiny new taps and the plumber, with the blunt pencil behind his ear, leaving the sighting mark on the wall; the

**170**

sighting mark that could still be seen to the left of one of the brackets. Imagined the whole house new and the wardrobe mirrors clear, with no silver bits showing. All things were without blemish once.

"What she said to me," he was saying. "You know, as though she really meant it. With real venom." He ran a hand through his hair, walked to the window. "I don't get it. I don't get it at all."

"You're not meant to get it, Adrian." A soft tumble of words like kittens in snow, words you could pick up and hold against your cheek. "Look, she's obviously going through some stuff with Phileda. Don't take it to heart."

In the far distance the telephone rang. The wire from the television aerial had come loose and rapped against the window. The world went on and there was no slowing any of it down. The noise seemed to jolt him from a waking sleep. He rubbed his eyes.

"I'd die if I lost her. Is that something you can understand?" He looked at me, as though seeing me for the first time. "Of course you can, what am I saying." And I was struck by the image of cattle rushing to a quarry edge and throwing themselves off; an image from a recurring dream. He put a hand to his brow. "Where's this taking me?" his voice, softer than I'd ever heard it. "I'd die if I lost her." Again. Each word a stone to swallow, hardening from the inside. I pulled Isabel's shirt out of my trousers, felt the release of skin, cool air on warm, the knot inside like the innards of a golf ball, miles of knottiness. Traitors, all of them. The chain and its pendant slid to the floor.

"Adrian," I put out my hand. It dipped into air, then touched solid, soft.

"Adrian, come close. Come here. Just to say I'm sorry. Sorry for what's happening." And I put my hands over his ears, squaring up his face to mine so that he wouldn't hear Isabel's footsteps on the stairs. He wouldn't hear them because he wasn't listening for them. But I was. I was listening for them in the way a dog listens for its owner's footsteps on a garden path, with every muscle keening. *One, two, three steps on stairs.* He didn't move. And with the pressure of my hands on his ears I brought down his head. *Ten, eleven, twelve steps on stairs.* I brought down his head to me. *Rattle of the door handle.* Lent inwards to him. *Scrape of door on boards.* And kissed. The peppery, boy taste of him. *Isabel.*

She was there looking at us and then she was not there. We both stared at the space where she had been in the doorway.

"Stay there," I said to Adrian.

He reached out with his fingers, said, "Is . . ." then sat down, hard, on the edge of the bed; his face vacant, disbelieving, like an acrobat who's missed the trapeze.

"Leave it to me. It's my fault. It's up to me to sort it out," I said. Invisible words; nothing. A strange, sweet pleasure like tasting a new kind of tropical fruit for the first time.

I left him sitting there, immobile with misery, and went after Isabel. The rain had stopped. Her steps were like animal tracks across the wet lawn. I followed. Even without the tracks I knew where to find her. It was obvious she'd run to the tree house that Geoffrey had built for her: that warm burrow of paternal love; her cheek remembering the scrape of his weekend stubble and the Arran twirl in his fisherman's jumper. A place where scraped knees were kissed better and tears rewarded by chocolate, and every fresh wish came true.

"I'd buy you the stars if I could," he'd said, with his nose in her newly washed hair. I imagined him stooping to tie her shoelace, calling her "sugar plum" and "his girl", and that if she was lucky, really lucky, a kiss would buy her a star swing by the arms.

The tree house sat low in the spreading branches of a yew tree on the other side of the walled garden. It had a ladder and feathered eaves and a door made of bark. I'd made holes in the roof by pulling off the felt to accelerate its decline; wouldn't rest until it was gone and couldn't provoke me any more. "Bloody squirrels," Popey had said, shaking his head furiously when he saw. He knew someone who had a lurcher. "I'll see to them," he'd said.

Through the open door I could see Isabel cupped in its dark interior. I called out but she didn't reply. I told her I was coming up; saw her shoes on the soaking boards as my head emerged at the top of the ladder — black ribbons instead of laces — the kind of easy style I could never achieve. She said nothing, only stared at the dripping walls. The smell of rotting wood like wet, burnt toast; a sodden poster on the wall of a rabbit and a kitten asleep together and, underneath, the words "Love is," the bottom half torn and on the floor the word, "friendship". At any moment I expected her to strike out, to whip me with her tongue, her hands, the flat side of her loathing, but she controlled herself by not looking at me. She kept her face to the wall.

"I used to love this place," she said sadly. "Dad built it for me. Did I tell you that? We used to have picnics here. I'd bring my bears and a plastic tea set, and he'd sit on a tiny chair and sip tea from a yellow cup, making a big show of holding it properly by the handle. I even had a little checked cloth for the table. Funny, I never remember Mum in here, only Dad, but memory can be selective, can't it?" She looked at me, finally. Her eyes were inscrutable, like gates she had closed on the poor.

"Isabel. It's not how it looks. I know what you're thinking but you must believe me, Adrian is not good enough for you."

Ignoring me, she continued: "Once I made soup out of dandelions and rainwater and Dad pretended to drink it. I thought I'd poisoned him because he started to choke. It was so real and I was so frightened. He writhed around on the floor with his hands at his throat and his face turning puce, and I really did believe I'd killed him. Then he sprang up, laughing, and I hit him and hit him because I loved him so much and I'd suddenly had a glimpse of what life would be like without him, the most awful emptiness." She rubbed her arm and then in a quiet hiss said: "Diane, you bitch. How could you?" The relief was immense; some real words after the sugar.

After a pause I said, "I know it would be easier for you to believe that I led Adrian astray up there. It's neater somehow when people revert to type. Humble is, as humble does. You think you took a gamble on me and it didn't pay off."

"I never said . . ."

"But the truth is often much harder to bear. I didn't make a move on Adrian. You must believe me. I've practically had to fight him off over the past few days." She shaded her eyes as though blinded by a bright light. "There's so much you don't know about him, Isabel. You're so honest and innocent and good. You don't know people like I know them."

She snorted and raised her eyes to the ceiling. "Diane, there's so much you don't know about me."

"Adrian is not to be trusted . . . in more ways than one."

"What do you mean?"

I turned away from her and pulled some bark off the wall. Underneath, a mass of woodlice, their armour-plated bodies scrambling over each other, desperate to regain the darkness. A breeze made the tree house sway and the wooden frame cracked as it tensed and relaxed. The word "friendship" flapped around on the floor like a fish in the bottom of a boat.

She said again, "What do you mean?"

"I mean, he's been taking things from the house."

"I don't believe you," she said quietly.

"I didn't think you would. But I knew I'd have to be the one to tell you."

She laughed. "How cheap can you get?" Her hand in her hair now, furiously pulling. "Don't give me that honest and innocent crap. You sleep with my boyfriend and, when I find out, you tell me you were doing me a favour because he's a thief." On her feet now, pacing the boards. A lit fuse, spitting and sparking, alive. What I'd have said; arch, sharp. Two girls in a subsiding tree house. A far point in the distance. I could just make out the shape of it, the shiny, metal finish of it, something hot enough to warm my hands around. The future.

"No, Isabel. You know that's not true. Anyway I can prove it. I'll show you. Come on, I'll show you if you don't believe me."

In her eyes anger was replaced by a fear of the unknown; the need to know a kind of gluttony. A moment of no words or action while she measured, in her mind's eye, the gorge she must leap across. *I'll show you.* Each word the butt of a rifle in the small of her back.

She swallowed hard. "Show me, then," she said.

# CHAPTER
# ELEVEN

And so we went. I led the way back though the garden, across the lawn and into the house. The hall, as I'd seen it many times before but different now, whiter — all things on the brink of change. On the stairs I turned to Isabel and put a finger to my lips: quiet. We stopped outside Adrian's door. I knocked softly. No sound from within. I opened the door and entered, but Isabel hesitated on the threshold. All the confidence money could buy had left her now and had been replaced by the insecurity of impending betrayal.

The room displayed all the signs of recent occupancy. By the bed, the inside of a stale glass of water encrusted with bubbles. Curtains half closed. Adrian's bag, still only half unpacked on the floor but sitting precisely, as though placed, in the middle of a rose on the carpet. Isabel looked drugged, like a bad photograph of herself, eyelids caught drooping in the click of the shutter. She came in and looked up at the ceiling, as though expecting something to fall onto her shoulders from a great height. I caught a glimpse of the purple hills between the gap in the curtains. It seemed impossible that another world outside this room existed.

She flinched when I moved towards the chest of drawers. It had gold swags for handles and the surface of the wood was so highly polished it looked artificial. I opened the second drawer down, rummaged among the jumpers for effect, stopped. Elongated the moment, tried to stretch it.

"See, what did I tell you? What more proof do you want?" We peered into the drawer like broody mothers into a cradle. I parted two sleeves for her to see. There was the Cooper, no bigger than my hand, the slight, insolent smile of the sitter staring back at us; the face displaying the smug certainty of the long dead. Isabel stared at the picture trying to comprehend, and while she did, I began to feel her fall away from me. I couldn't help but think of her in water, floating backwards, with bubbles rising from her mouth. Her eyes were two liquid pools of tears.

I thought I knew this part of the story, the part where she snatched the portrait from my hand and threw it against the wall, and the tortoiseshell frame broke into tiny, splintered strips of colour; the part where an agonised moan was the only sound she was capable of making. But I didn't know the whole story, even though I gave it life, because I didn't foresee the panic, the sheer nervous panic that mutilated the features of her face. And the other: the something I was supposed to know but didn't, the part I'd overlooked. That missing piece of information.

Then she was gone and I was left standing alone in the overly warm room, listening to the water bubbling in the radiators. The pieces of frame were scattered over the bed, the broken glass in murderously glinting shards peeping out from between the tumbled sheets. A coldness, like being touched through plastic gloves, crossed my skin. And suddenly the rest of the day was no longer there to be stretched into, like every day before this one. It had changed.

There was only one person who could explain things fully to me now. Moments later, I was striding into Phileda's room. She was lying on the bed, still in her dressing-gown. I noticed that the pattern on the dressing-gown was made up of tiny linked fish with open mouths. "Tell me what I've missed?" I said. "What you should have told me."

But she was too wrapped up in her own world to want to talk to me. No, it was more than that. She seemed sealed in, like a blue pattern under a thick glaze. There was an open bottle of tablets by the bedside. She turned over on her side away from me.

"Phileda," I said, "this is really important. There's something you've not told me about Isabel. What did she mean when she said you were obviously cruel?"

"Don't. Don't," she moaned.

"You must tell me."

"Why must I tell you?"

"Because you tell Amelia everything, that's why. Remember, we have no secrets. Secrets are bad for us."

"Amelia?" she said. "Amelia? Where's Amelia? Dear Amelia, you're here."

"I'm here," I said. She turned over to face me.

"Yes, of course you are. All grown up now." Her hand reached out to stroke my cheek.

"Now tell me, what did Isabel mean?"

"Oh, silly old Isabel. Silly old muffin."

"Phileda, concentrate." She hinged her hands in the middle and made them flap. The pale fingers brushed the underside of my chin. She made a wooing sound like a child's impression of a ghost. And then stopped and looked me straight in the eye.

"We bought her from the stork, of course."

I ran like someone who doesn't run very often, as though I was imitating an athlete with arms pumping up and down. I saw myself running down the drive and back again, across the front lawn to the courtyard, to the old laundry: "Flash Washes Whiter" still in the window. It was as though I was directing myself in a film. When I thought this, I stopped running.

I couldn't find Isabel and I was out of breath. I'd looked all over the house but there was no sign of her. The rain had stopped completely. There was even some blue appearing between the clouds. The earth smelt darkly of rot. The ground was covered in small, yellow leaves but there was no tree anywhere that had such leaves. Neither was it autumn. All the blossoms drooped or were flattened. The fallen petals bruised easily, their journey to the ground was written on them like a memoir.

The meaning of Phileda's words. It all fitted into place. Adopt: to receive the child of another and treat it as your own. Isabel was recompense for Amelia. Substitute: to put in the place of another. Cuckoo: a small bird of the genus *Cuculus*, deriving its name from its note. Something told me the winning and the losing was over. We were all but a fraction of the whole. Isabel had been found and lost by two fathers, and lost again by Adrian: a scab pulled off an unripe wound.

I found that I was running again, but this time so fast I didn't notice myself. I had to find Isabel. I wanted to ask her if two mothers were better than one because one mother had not been enough for me.

I went down to the apple room. On my way I passed the field where the horses lived. But there were no horses and the gate was open, and the mud around the gate had been ground up and slipped into. Phileda's words seemed to filter through the mud like bubbles, impossible to keep down: "We did a very bad thing, didn't we, burning Isabel's papers?"

"Yes, Phileda, we did a very bad thing."

"Why was it a very bad thing?"

"It was a very bad thing because the papers and toys were all Isabel had left of her life before Critchley."

"You mean, before the stork came and brought her to us?"

"Yes, before the stork came and brought her to you."

When I looked, the horses had gone. My head felt heavy. I began to hum. It took the loneliness out of my head. Must find Isabel. There was a trail of hoof marks out of the gate. I followed them. In places the hooves had come down so heavily that the white stone showed through the mud, like bone when the meat's taken off. There were patterns to be seen, beautiful abstract patterns. I was sweating inside my clothes; soon the insects would notice and would suck on the rich gravy of me. The mud had covered my feet and made lifting them heavy.

I followed the lane that skirted the back of Critchley. The hoof prints reappeared and disappeared according to the hardness of the ground. Where it was soft there was always one print stretching ahead, the other three catching up and further behind; the same pattern again: Hester following Darius. I could hear Adrian calling Isabel, then me, then Isabel again, muffled but close, like he was shouting from behind a raised towel at the seaside, the trees giving the same effect. I didn't answer. I pulled a leaf out of my hair instead. The canopy of branches was a consolation. The horses had moved fast, as though urged by an instinct to flee. Here the lane bent round and up, between two gateposts said to be monoliths. They were soft and pale, as if they'd been cast from milk, full of air pockets and the lichen that had sprouted from within. This lane, I knew, led to the quarry, now disused but with the gouges in the rock face still apparent. The lane lessened and became a track, weaving its way between the gorse bushes to the top of the quarry, where the young-stubbled grass tickled the earth's face.

I climbed. A breeze whipped over the brow and cuffed my hair. I saw Hester with her head down, cropping grass; the underside of her stomach was mud-matted from last night's roll. Being here felt dangerous but I wasn't sure why. If I hadn't wanted to speak to Isabel so badly, I would have turned around and gone back. Something she'd said ages ago, I'd just remembered. She'd said that when she passed people in the street she could sense who would die before her, and for this reason it seemed like the most extraordinary privilege to see those people laugh or eat ice cream, or put on mascara or kiss, because in her mind they were already ghosts. It made you love them instead of hate them, she'd said. The feeling that you could reach out and put your hand right through them. Even without looking over the edge of the quarry, I knew I would never speak to Isabel again. Just before it happened, Hester looked up. A weight in my stomach fell. In a nearby country lane a motorbike backfired. It sounded like a whiplash, something cruel.

Weight. Wait. As light as sound, as light as light, as breath. Weightlessness. What diving off a high board into a canyon of cool air felt like, when the globe in the very centre of your stomach stayed still but the rest of you moved. Falling through the bird-warmed air. Slow. Motion. Sky that smelled of line-dried washing. The drag of gravity, like being vacuumed out of space. What it felt like to fall over the edge; on the edge of a whole different story. Her beating heart. Mine. The senses she would no longer sense. Senseless.

There were slips of mud where Darius hesitated, then panicked on the lip of a great leap; striding out into nothing, unable to pull himself back in time. The crack of the backfiring motorbike a hoo-ha in his brain. His body floating, then shifting, an equine statue come to life. His hooves pawing the weather now, impatient for his last gallop into the last draught of the gorse-seasoned breeze.

I ran to where the stone of the quarry had been sheared away a long time ago, where the chisels and the hammers gouged new contours in the mountain and nature had since healed up the wound with a scab of moss; and I looked over. There were two shapes on the ground, a long way down. I stretched out my arm and covered them up with my hand. But I couldn't keep my hand there for ever. For a moment I thought I could follow. But really I was just giving in to the thrill of thinking I could step off. I was not who she was, after all. No, I was not. I was not half the person.

I took my hand away and the shapes came back, and I thought I saw animals crowding round her, rabbits and deer, like a scene from *Bambi*. Even in death she could charm the birds out of the trees, the animals from their lairs. I ran down into the bowl of the quarry. I didn't want the animals to touch her. But they were not animals. They were tumbled rocks and bits of plastic bag snagged on fern. Except for a leg that was bent oddly like an icing squiggle on a cake, she lay unbroken on the ground. I recalled the pigeon in St Mark's Square. A crown of blood emerged from behind her head. It was dark, distinctive, rich, like ink. Her elbow was raised on a pillow of white stone.

The huge bulk of the horse lay nearby. Her fingers were still entwined in his mane; white knuckles where she'd tried to pull him back. Now she was connected in some unfathomable way to the beauties of nature: the part that curled leaves and sharpened the fronds of fern. To my surprise, Darius's leg twitched. He wasn't dead. He began to kick like a dreaming dog. I watched, paralysed by a fascination for the macabre and the curiously beautiful: the big horse and the small girl lying side by side, the picturesqueness of it.

There was a noise behind me. I heard Old Popey's wheezy breaths coming up the track and his shouts in between: "What's happened, eh? What's happened?" And then he was beside me, his gun on his arm from shooting moles on the top lawn, a roll-up behind his ear for later. His later would be different now. There would be shockwaves through the village and questions, all the whys and ifs to come. He knelt down and touched Isabel's cheek: gnarled fingers on white skin — the only time he'd been allowed. He consumed the tragedy in silence, as though he was eating it in secret, forcing it down, gluttonously, and yet with a hint of self-disgust. He wiped away a tear with the back of his hand. The sunburned skin on his face like crackling on pork, with the odd hard hair sprouting through. He took off his coat and moved to lay it across her face but I stopped him, thinking of the sweat in the lining, the armpits and the open pores. Then the sun came out and made everything glisten, made everything seem like new and the day went on just as before.

Darius moved again. Popey looked carefully at the horse, his eyes expertly assessing the damage. He moved towards it, stroked its neck, clicked his gun and shot it in the head. It heaved, it breathed its last, and died. It was over. I saw that now. But precisely what that meant I did not know.

# CHAPTER
# TWELVE

I open my eyes and am surprised to find myself in the present. Now is current, real, a pinch on the arm. A whole winter and summer have passed. It is autumn again. I am back at the beginning. And it seems more important than the end. The sun is bouncing off the brown fields. The windows are reflecting it; somewhere, it blinds a driver momentarily. The pheasants are out in it. For the first time in days their feathers are properly dry.

Months have passed, whole seasons have passed, since Isabel's funeral. On that day it threatened rain. The clouds were grey, dirty-looking; it seemed impossible that something as clean as rain could be held inside so grimy a casing. The church path was newly tarmacked, the tar like fallen soot where it had crumbled at the edges. We walked up the path, the coffin ahead of us, perched on the shoulders of four short men. The smoothness of the box, the wedge shape of it if you turned it on its side — a wedge to keep doors open, for death and its clutter closed none. Nobody could bring themselves to look at it.

Phileda's arrangement went unseen, though everyone afterwards said how beautiful it was, how perfect, without saying why or what flowers had been used. Phileda kept her arm linked in mine. I'd grown, she'd shrunk. I loved myself in black; caught sight of myself in the ripple of a brass plate, my veil (yes, my veil!) graphing my face with feigned solemnity. A hymn, all happy hymns, a mistake in my opinion, bore us up the aisle. And it struck me that Isabel's death had forged a kind of marriage between Phileda and myself: a wedding and a funeral rolled into one.

We took our seats in the family pew, Adrian behind. I sensed the bulk of Geoffrey moving up the aisle and I shivered remembering the closeness of him, the sheer weight of him above. I heard the priest speak of the comfort of the church at times like these; our dear sister Isabel and what the loss meant, that we would all be stronger people in the end. There was sniffing from behind, a cough, the fabric shush of people moving inside unused-to clothes. Another hymn, then Geoffrey got up and walked towards the pulpit to read the address. Phileda raised her eyes, seeing but unseeing, her face the colour of a pill, as though all that was on the inside had moved through to the outside. Geoffrey cleared his throat, glanced at his notes, then put them aside. I imagined his face was an icy crust and my eyes burned through him to get to the fish beneath.

"How much Isabel overcame in her short life," he began. "She was an example to us all. She knew what it was to suffer and to overcome hardships. Before she came to Critchley, her life in a children's home was not easy. It was a little-known fact that she was adopted. In the face of adversity, she made the best of everything. She turned every setback into an advantage."

The privileges of poverty were no longer mine. They now belonged to Isabel. She had usurped me as the urchin child; she had denied me even this. I hoped his eulogy would soon be over. My mind drifted off to the puddings I would cook, the dog I would own (brown with a white blaze down its front), the summer holiday that would stretch on and on: the rest of my life.

"It was truth and honesty that set Isabel apart." His voice with iron filings in it; different from how I remembered. There was a smell of candlewax and damp plaster, mothballs from winter coats. Geoffrey's eyes were now on me. "And true regard for her friends." Suddenly the atmosphere had changed; I sensed a drum roll in the air. He paused for effect. I began to feel uncomfortable. I focused on the polished head of a pelican halfway up the pulpit. Then came his words, quietly spoken but deadly, like silent bullets aimed to wound. "Despite her hardships, envy was not a word in her vocabulary. In this regard, she differed from her closest contemporaries."

I met his eye; our stares duelled in the godly glow. Never had I felt so aware of myself: the rankness of me; though the feeling was not without a certain sweetness. The rest I didn't hear. Geoffrey's veiled judgement of me stuck like a catchphrase in my throat. I wanted to shout, to do something sudden, to prove I was alive and killing time in a valuable way, not it killing me with the blows of its threadbare wings. I looked down. My fingers had been busy. The black sweep of my coat was covered with the Order of Service torn to tiny shreds like confetti. Then I remembered that I would be going home to Critchley and Geoffrey would be going back to his rented accommodation on the Edgware Road. I felt the glow again and smiled savagely at him.

All good things must come to an end. But what of bad things? Do bad things then enjoy the pleasure of eternity? I spend a moment wondering if the answer to that question is important. I decide no, and look out of the window.

Adrian and Phileda are walking in the garden. It is his second visit in a month. She walks beside him like a patient. She points at a thrush as it lifts from the ground with a worm in its mouth. They laugh when the worm is dropped. She takes delight in the small banalities of nature. It is the only time she comes alive. It is human exchanges that deaden her. He motions to a bench that sits in a carved-out bit of high hedge. There are leaves on the seat of it. Phileda picks one up, inspects it carefully and then sits in the space it has made. She passes the leaf to Adrian. They talk about it. Something about it must be funny because they laugh. I will be happier when he leaves. There is a rhythm to our days that visitors disrupt.

Things are different now between Adrian and me. He visited Critchley a few months after the funeral. Phileda asked him to stay to dinner and afterwards offered him a bed to save him the drive home. He accepted. After dinner, I was reading in the drawing

**189**

room. Phileda had gone to bed. Adrian came in and asked if he could join me.

I said, "Of course," but I did mind. I liked to keep the quiet hours after dinner to myself. He poured himself a drink — another presumption that irked me. He handed me one too, then threw his big, flat body onto the cushions of the sofa opposite. He said nothing for a while but I knew there was something on his mind. He breathed noisily through his nose, like a racehorse impatient to be off. I knew he couldn't find the start of what he wanted to say. He swallowed his drink. I heard it hitting the back of his throat.

"Adrian, is there anything troubling you?" I said. "Anything I can help you with?" He smiled, moved by my consideration.

"There's something I need to ask you, Diane. Something I need to get off my chest before I feel we can move our friendship forward."

I smiled, too, at this, though he would not have recognised it as a smile. I sipped my drink: metallic; brown coins dissolved in water.

"I need to know what happened. I need to know why Isabel ran away like that? I can't sleep at night thinking about it. Were we responsible?" He ran his hands through his hair, the shine on his curls was bright, the way candlelight catches in metal. "Were we in any way to blame for what happened?"

I put my drink down and leaned forward. There was a stillness in the room. It was full of the mournful presence of books unopened and unread. Adrian wore jeans and the jacket of a pinstripe suit; my eyes traced

**190**

the outline of its collar. He asked me whether I'd spoken to Isabel after she'd seen us together in my room. There was a tremor in his voice, and I thought of moles and how sensitive they were to the vibration of approaching footsteps. "I must ask you this. I must know," he kept saying, with his head in his hands and his elbows pushing into his knees.

I told him I'd spoken to Isabel in the tree house an hour before ... and the sentence hung there, unfinished, bloated with meaning and the dark space that death left behind. "Isabel trusted me," I said. "She didn't for a moment think there was anything between us, Adrian, because there so obviously wasn't. I told her how upset you were after the argument. She was pleased that I consoled you. I suppose it's flattering and at the same time terrifying to think that something we've said or done could have the power to cause the death of another person. But, really, what happened had nothing to do with you. It was an accident. Yes, Isabel was angry but not because of something you had done. She was angry with her mother for burning the papers in the attic. Phileda, as you know, will never forgive herself. It's her we should console. It's why I'm still here. I don't see it as a sacrifice. I see it as my duty. It's the one thing I'm still able to give."

There was a dim glow in his eyes, like a light seen through mist far out to sea. He was fighting back tears. It was easier for him to go on blaming himself than to accept that Isabel hadn't cared about seeing us together in my room that day.

"Isabel found commitment difficult," I said. "Perhaps it was because she was adopted. It's why she kept you at arm's length. But she did love you in her own way. Just not in the way that you loved her." And I was surprised how little I felt; how little those words gave me. It was how a killer must feel when killing becomes mechanical: joyless, withered. I watched his eyes for signs of slippage. His face was still and sad like a carnival mask with a downward smile, as though weights were pulling at the corners of his mouth. The lamplight dipped and flared.

"You understand everything, Diane," he said quietly. His fingers scratched at a small mark on his trousers. Then he caught sight of the frameless Cooper back on the wall behind my head. "We never did tell her about that, did we? She'd have enjoyed that. It would have amused her."

I got up and moved to the window. He finished his drink. I kept my eyes fixed on a distant house light. I heard his feet falling through the rug as he walked towards me. There was a breeze outside. The light blinked behind the moving trees. His knees creaked and hit the floorboards as he knelt down behind me. I felt his hands lift up the back of my skirt. His head fell against my bare legs. And for one paralysing moment I closed my eyes and let my hands slip away from the rails, let myself soak in the hotness of his touch. It took me to a cushioned place. His lips were on the back of my legs; his arms around them like a lasso. I gave way. I was a line of traffic yielding to the oncoming flow. Moments passed and I thought how different life might have been. I had a glimpse of an unlived memory in which Adrian filled the space at my side. I was a leaf lying in grass. I was a nut safe in its shell. We held hands and went for walks in another world, where streams ran uphill and the sun burned beneath our feet.

My eyes snapped open. Adrian was murmuring something into the back of my legs. His grip tightened. I realised with a cold stab that they weren't kisses I could feel — they were tears — his eyelashes were fanning tears across the tautness of my skin. He was calling softly for Isabel. He was whimpering like a small, hungry creature that's been left behind in the nest: "Isabel, Isabel, Isabel."

I said nothing. I'd made a mistake. It wouldn't happen again. I left him kneeling on the floor and walked out of the room. I had melted momentarily but now I had reformed again in glass: I was full of imperfections and all the harder for a second firing.

When Phileda and I are alone, it's like it was when Isabel was away at college: the two of us expectant of nothing, content beneath the gloss of meals, the garden, the slow changes in the weather. She is content with her Amelia. Phileda sometimes asks when Isabel will be coming back and I haven't the heart to disillusion her. I haven't the heart!

Phileda and Adrian are in the garden. I watch them from the window. Adrian looks up at the house. I can't stop him visiting. But he is no threat to my position in the house. It is Phileda he comes to see. His face is older; a year older in fact. I imagine he's thinking about

Isabel, wondering if she's ghosting the interior of the house. His eyes pause on the windows of her room. It's hard not to think about her: she's more here now than when she was alive. I think about her all the time — the sexiness of death — what she knows and we don't; the power of that.

Phileda stands up and takes a piece of bread from her pocket. She crumbles it into tiny pieces, "For the birds," her lips say. Her face is blank but there's a trace of suffering in the lines around her eyes. The thrush is nowhere to be seen. The crumbs drop onto the lawn but most fall into her shoes, down the sides and over the buckles. She doesn't notice. She breaks the bread into ever-smaller pieces, and I think of the crumbs lying beneath the arch of her foot and how with enough moisture and the kneading action of her steps they will return again to dough.

She relies on me for everything. On good days she is like a fearless kitten that would swim across a pond if I let her. Her barometer is stuck on extremes; there is nothing in the middle with Phileda. And yet some seed of self-preservation prevents absolute severance from reality. She always returns from behind the dark veil. I manage her with kindness. It is the best way. She craves sentient experience: last week I found her in the potting shed with her hands rummaging beneath the compost in the propagator. She looked like a child, forgiven after punishment. The scent of hot, ripening tomatoes was almost overwhelming. She raised her hands carefully from the soil and on the tips of every other finger a seedling quivered. She smiled at me and I envied her arrival at such a simple place. We returned the seedlings to the squashy soil and she watered them with a child's watering can. She had on little red wellington boots. And I knew, in a way, I had forsaken another mother in adopting the role myself. I led her back to the house and we made cakes, and she sat on Isabel's stool and licked the mixture off her fingers. She is happy existing in her own faraway place.

I go out almost never. There is no need. Popey delivers our groceries. We live simply, without waste or ostentation. There is something liberating about living behind the high, protecting walls of Critchley — a dislocation from society, that is in itself strengthening.

Every day would be glorious if I knew I did not have unfinished business to attend to. It is to do with Isabel. It is a feeling that lately has begun to niggle and worm its way to the surface. In my dreams, I see myself spitting out maggots and sometimes choking on them. They crawl from my nose and ears, and one morning last week I woke up with something like soil in my eyes. It is this: I envy the way Isabel died and the feeling pushes me to darker thoughts every day.

Sometimes I go back to the quarry to see if I can see her there. A small posy of flowers anoints the spot where she fell. They are always seasonal flowers: sometimes snowdrops or bluebells; in winter, even mistletoe or holly. I've tried more than once to clear them away but each time they return, more beautiful, more delicately arranged, so strong is the cult of Isabel — what death has done for her.

I reach out and touch the space she fell through. The emptiness of the place is big enough to stand inside and yet she lives in everything that moves. She has not fallen behind the back of gone. Isabel is here. She walks in and out of people's dreams with ease now. She walks through walls, slides under doors; has become a scent that lingers in wool. Knots of her hair have been cleaned from brushes, forever to be preserved in the clot-encrusted reliquary of the heart. The beautiful, tragic, brown-eyed girl has become a story and the land weeps for her. She will never be forgotten.

Death has given her something else I want. There is an art to dying well: I will better her death for beauty alone; it is a point in the distance I hunger for. It will take some beating. But beat her I will. Because now I have plenty of time to work out how.

# The Villa in Italy

## Elizabeth Edmondson

An irresistible invitation to a magical place.

Four strangers are summoned to the Villa Dante, a beautiful but abandoned house above the Ligurian coast. Each has been named in the will of the intriguing Beatrice Malaspina, but not one of them knows who she is or what the connection might be. Delia, an opera singer robbed of her voice; George, an atom scientist unable to face what his skills have created; Marjorie, a detective novelist with writer's block; and Lucius, a Boston banker whose personal life is in chaos.

As they wait to find out why they're all there, the villa begins to work its seductive magic. Amongst the faded frescoes, overgrown garden and magnificent mediaeval tower, four determined characters slowly begin to change — the sorrow of their wartime experiences growing into hope. But the mysterious Beatrice has a devastating secret to reveal that will affect them all . . .

ISBN 978-0-7531-7890-4 (hb)
ISBN 978-0-7531-7891-1 (pb)

# Over

## Margaret Forster

Louise, a mother and primary school teacher, is trying to hold herself together after her teenage daughter dies in mysterious circumstances. She's trying to get on with life, trying to understand not "what happened", but what is happening to them all in the wake of the accident, and why.

Don, her husband, cannot accept that his child's death might have been an accident. He wants someone to blame, becoming obsessive in his quest for a reason, travelling restlessly, neglecting work and family in pursuit of the "truth". Their other children handle the tragedy better than their parents. What they can't deal with is the way their parents are tearing each other and the family apart.

**ISBN 978-0-7531-7894-2 (hb)**
**ISBN 978-0-7531-7895-9 (pb)**

# Glass Houses

## Sandra Howard

It is Sunday morning after a General Election and Victoria James is at home awaiting a call from Downing Street. Part of her is desperate for the telephone to ring — but a small part of her is willing it to remain silent, mindful of the lasting impact a promotion could have on her husband and daughter.

When Victoria receives the summons, high office does indeed await her: she is appointed Minister of State for Housing — and life as she, Barney and 16-year-old Nattie know it will never be the same. From the outset, her political mettle will be tested to the utmost. As a young, attractive female Minister, she will be living firmly in the public eye, challenged in her views at every turn. But nothing prepares her for what ultimately throws her off-balance: a love affair with a married man so well known that it can only be a matter of time before everyone knows their secret . . .

**ISBN 978-0-7531-7882-9 (hb)**
**ISBN 978-0-7531-7883-6 (pb)**

# Keeping Faith

## Jodi Picoult

For the second time in her marriage, Mariah White catches her husband with another woman, and Faith, their seven-year-old daughter, witnesses every painful minute. In the aftermath of a sudden divorce, Mariah struggles with depression and Faith begins to confide in an imaginary friend.

At first, Mariah dismisses these exchanges as a child's imagination. But when Faith starts reciting passages from the Bible, develops stigmata and begins to perform miraculous healings, Mariah wonders if her daughter — a girl with no religious background — might indeed be seeing God. As word spreads and controversy heightens, Mariah and Faith are besieged by believers and disbelievers alike, caught in a media circus that threatens what little stability they have left.

**ISBN 978-0-7531-7830-0 (hb)**
**ISBN 978-0-7531-7831-7 (pb)**